SECRET OF THE RING

Released from Newgate jail, Dick Palmer, the son of a notorious highwayman, rides off to seek a new life outside London. However, he arrives at the village of High Beach to rest at the Black Horse Inn — and is framed for murder. Jeanette, the innkeeper's daughter, aids his escape, but like his father, he is forced to become a highwayman. Fighting to clear his name, he and Jeanette then become enmeshed in a sinister mystery involving an earlier murder . . .

JOHN RUSSELL FEARN

SECRET OF
THE RING

Complete and Unabridged

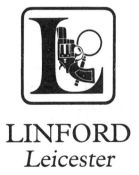

LINFORD
Leicester

First published in Great Britain

First Linford Edition
published 2008

British Library CIP Data

Fearn, John Russell, *1908 – 1960*
    Secret of the ring.—Large print ed.—
Linford mystery library
    1. Detective and mystery stories
    2. Large type books
    I. Title
    823.9′12 [F]

ISBN 978–1–84782–409–7

Published by
F. A. Thorpe (Publishing)
Anstey, Leicestershire

Set by Words & Graphics Ltd.
Anstey, Leicestershire
Printed and bound in Great Britain by
T. J. International Ltd., Padstow, Cornwall

This book is printed on acid-free paper

Foreword

On the morning of April 7th, 1739, Dick Turpin, the notorious highwayman, was hanged at York at the age of 32.

This story deals with his son, also named Dick. He was nine years old at the time of his father's death. Dick's mother, Mary, the year before had changed to her mother-in-law's maiden name of Palmer, for the wild exploits of her husband had made the change necessary.

Dick Palmer grew up in Hampstead. He was a fair-haired highly-strung youth and when he was 14, his mother died. Dick at once became restless, for the village was now a place of sad memories. One night he crept from his home and set out for London.

Little is known of Dick Palmer's earlier life in the city. It is believed he obtained employment with a tailor in Fleet Street, but he did not stay there long — his restless nature kept him on the move. At the age of 19 he fell in with a gang of thieves, but they were soon apprehended and Dick was sentenced to a year's imprisonment. He was confined in the grim Newgate jail and it was there that he met Jack Pale, a noted highwayman.

Pale was awaiting execution. The two became friendly, Pale finding the youth good company. But they were not to know each other very long, for Pale's day of execution was fixed and soon approached. The night before he was taken to Tyburn, the highwayman handed his young friend a note.

'Here, Dick,' he said, 'here is a parting gift — she is the only thing I have ever loved.'

Palmer, upon reading the note later, discovered that the highwayman had left him his chestnut mare. Written in almost illegible letters, the note told him to go to the White Bear Inn, Drury Lane, and ask for Harry Peggott, the ostler. A few words at the bottom of the note were addressed to Peggott.

Dick was released three months later and he borrowed a sum of money from an acquaintance and then followed the directions in Jack Pale's note. He accosted Harry Peggott in the yard at the back of the inn. Peggott, a fat youth, read the letter out loud to himself. When he had finished he eyed Palmer a little suspiciously, but at last he seemed satisfied and told Dick to follow him across to the stables.

The ostler went inside and passed down to the far end. A beautiful chestnut mare stood in the corner stall eating hay, her flanks glistening in the light from a horn lantern standing on a ledge nearby.

'That be 'er,' said Harry Peggott.

'That one?' gasped Palmer with delight.

'Yes, an' you be lucky, as I sees you appreciate. She's as fine a courser as ever I've seen, an' that's a fact!'

Dick Palmer thrilled with excitement as he gazed upon the mare. She was undoubtedly a magnificent steed — the breadth of her chest, the clean, shapely lines of her limbs, the swan-like arch of her neck — all proclaimed the excellence of her pedigree.

'What is her name?' Dick asked.

'Jack Pale called 'er Red Ruby,' the ostler replied.

Dick stepped over to the mare and fingered her thick russet mane. Red Ruby turned and nuzzled her nose into the boy's hand with a low whinny of pleasure, and it was at that moment, as he gazed upon the smooth lines of the chestnut mare, that Dick Palmer came to his decision.

He would leave London — leave the great city with its sordid, teeming life — and set out for the wide open country. Then, in some distant place, he could start life anew. At the thought Palmer's eyes shone with excitement. Yes, he would leave now, directly he was mounted.

Harry Peggott had already started saddling the mare and in a few moments he led her out into the yard. He held the reins as Dick mounted. The boy swung into the saddle, hardly crediting his amazing luck. He had little expected Jack Pale to own such a fine steed as this. Anxiously Palmer grasped the reins, terrified that Peggott might suddenly order him to dismount. He nodded casually to the ostler, spurred the horse gently forward and trotted out across the yard, expecting any moment to be recalled.

'Farewell!' cried Peggott.

Dick turned quickly and waved back to him, and then he had passed around the corner of the inn and at once he broke into a canter. He was off! His heart filled with joy as he felt the easy, steady, powerful movements of Red Ruby beneath him. They passed swiftly down the road and headed North out of the city.

And so it was on the afternoon of June 25th, 1750, at the age of 20, Dick Palmer, the son of Dick Turpin, rode out of London in search of adventure.

1

Twilight spread gently over the dark green expanse of Epping Forest as Dick Palmer cantered along the road towards the village of High Beach.

Dusk had already fallen beneath the silent trees and, but for the sudden movement of some forest animal as it scurried away from the sound of Red Ruby's clattering hoofs, a peaceful stillness reigned. Patches of grey light lay here and there between the cart ruts where the rays of the moon filtered through the thick foliage overhead.

Dick was content and at peace with the world and he rejoiced in the deep silence that lay around him. He rode his horse well and Red Ruby stepped out, responding with alacrity to her master's touch.

The boy's forehead was serene and as he rode his curls of fair hair bounced up and down upon his broad shoulders. He wore a long blue coat edged with yellow braid, a blue waist-coat elaborately embroidered with yellow silk, and grey breeches enclosed in high, stout riding boots. The top two buttons of his waistcoat were unfastened displaying his frilled shirt, and above was a small cravat. Over all Palmer wore a black cloak.

At first sight he might have been taken for a gentleman of some wealth, but on closer inspection the frayed edges and worn cloth of his coat and waistcoat were revealed.

Through the trees ahead of him Dick espied a yellow light. He must be nearing High Beach. It was here, he had been told, there was an inn that provided excellent fare. As he drew closer Palmer saw that the light came from a small cottage standing back from the highway. Three horsemen suddenly appeared galloping towards him from the village beyond. Dick eased his horse into the side of the road to enable them to pass, but the newcomers turned off and rode up to the front of the cottage.

A small knot of people was gathered at the door and the sound of murmuring voices floated to Palmer's ear. The three horsemen dismounted and one of them, a tall, dark, well-dressed man, strode towards the cottage. The group of people at the door parted and the murmur ceased as the visitor hurried inside.

Palmer rode quietly across the sward in front of the cottage, dismounted, tethered Red Ruby to a trunk of a tree, and joined the group at the door. The two other horsemen did not notice him for they were watching the cottage with great interest. A labourer, standing at the side of Dick Palmer, looked up at him.

' 'Tis old Sally Burke that used to work at the Squire's,' he confided. 'She be at 'er last breath.'

Dick shook his head sadly. 'Who is the gentleman that's just arrived?' he asked.

'That's Squire Penfield — nice of 'im to come.'

Palmer nodded and watched the scene curiously through the low doorway. An old, grey-haired woman lay on a wooden bedstead, covered by a few thin blankets. She was restless and the light from the candle on the table by the bed lit up her twitching, wizened features.

The Squire bent over her and the old woman opened her eyes and saw him and suddenly she raised herself up from the bed.

'Ah!' she croaked, staring intently at him with her burning eyes.

She beckoned to him to draw closer and, when he had done so, she began to speak in a low, trembling voice. The people at the door craned their necks forward trying to hear what she had to say, but only a faint, droning whisper reached their ears.

The old woman suddenly stopped speaking and fell back on the pillow, breathing hard. The Squire straightened and Dick, for one moment, thought he saw a smile upon his lips. He turned away from the old woman and walked quickly towards the door, and as he passed by Palmer heard him mutter: 'At last — it's mine!' He joined the two men standing outside with the horses and the three of them mounted, rode out onto the highway and galloped back towards the village.

The small group of spectators, finding now nothing of further interest, but already having plenty of news to gossip about, gradually dispersed, shaking their heads sorrowfully.

Palmer returned to Red Ruby, who was pawing the ground impatiently. He mounted, rode out to the highway and entered the village. He pulled his horse to a halt on the edge of the green and gazed around. The cottage lights twinkled against the background of the dark forest, and over all there lay a peaceful silence.

It was in this neighbourhood, Dick reflected, that many of his father's daring hold-ups were committed and somewhere, deep in the forest, was the cave Dick Turpin and Bob King had used as their headquarters. Palmer stared about the village with a certain reverence, reliving many of the tales he had heard of his father's reckless exploits.

Over to his right he saw a well-lighted house and, guessing this to be the Black Horse, he spurred Red Ruby towards it. As he approached he saw that a number of men were sitting at the tables on the cobbled stones at the front of the inn. The Black Horse itself was a dark, squat building, the upper windows almost hidden by long, frowning eaves. By the side and behind the inn was a cobbled yard, surrounded by low outhouses.

Palmer rode into the yard, Red Ruby's hoofs making a loud clatter upon the stones. As he dismounted a door opened in one of the outhouses and a small, fair youth with wide, brown eyes stared across at him.

'Come, ostler,' cried Dick, 'we are thirsty.'

The youth moved away from the door, still gazing curiously at Palmer and the big, sleek chestnut mare. He took the bridle and turned and confronted Palmer with his big, round eyes.

'You're a foreigner?' he challenged, in a high, sing-song voice.

Dick Palmer nodded, dismounted, and awaited further questioning. There was none, however, and the ostler led Red Ruby away into the stable. Palmer grunted and made his way around to the front of the inn and sat down at an empty table. A squat, black-haired man appeared. Dick ordered a tankard of ale and a meal and informed the landlord he would sit outside until the latter was prepared.

The ale soon arrived and Palmer took a copious draught for he was thirsty. Replacing the tankard upon the table he settled back against the wall and gazed out across the green. Except for a few domestic noises issuing from the doorway of the inn, the whole village lay under a mantle of sombre quietness.

Dick was tired and he spread himself out and relaxed. At last he lifted his tankard again. He pushed back his curls and turned to inspect the man at the next table. The latter was a thin, pinched-faced individual, from what Dick could see of him, for his large hat was pulled well down over his brow, throwing a deep shadow across his features.

Palmer was about to lean across and pass the time of day, as becomes a good traveller, when he felt a light tap upon his shoulder. Glancing up he beheld a flabby, pockmarked face staring down upon him.

Dick jumped to his feet. 'Simon

Beckley,' he cried in surprise. 'How come you to these parts?' Dick remembered Beckley well — they had met one night in a London tavern when Beckley was consorting with a gang of thieves.

The fellow had just stepped out of the inn and now he glanced about him nervously. The thin, pinched-faced man on the other side of the door had turned and looked the other way. Beckley glanced at Palmer again.

'Dick,' he gasped in a terrified tone, 'I am in fear of my life — quick, I must tell you — let us go inside!'

Palmer stared at him in amazement, but Beckley tugged at his arm insistently and he followed his friend into the Black Horse Inn. As Dick Palmer crossed the threshold, the pinched-faced man got up and walked off down the road.

Simon Beckley led the way down a narrow passage between the bar rooms to the rear of the inn. Palmer followed close behind, curious to know the reason for his friend's frightened behaviour. They turned a corner and Beckley opened a door on the right. The passage, Dick noted, ended in a low doorway — leading, most likely, out into the yard.

Beckley had entered a small, sparsely furnished room. A window on the left looked out over the yard. He hurried across and looked out anxiously. Seeming satisfied he returned and lit the candle on the table. He then rang the hand bell hanging on the wall and in a few moments a grey-haired woman appeared.

'What you want?' she asked.

Beckley motioned Palmer to sit down and then ordered some ale. The woman disappeared and Beckley sat down at the table and waited silently until she returned. When she did appear again she was carrying two brimming tankards of ale. She placed them on the table before Palmer and his friend and waited patiently whilst Beckley delved in his capacious pockets for a coin. He found one, paid the woman and then waved her away.

When the door had closed, Beckley grabbed his tankard and thirstily poured the liquid down his throat, spilling some at the same time down the front of his frilled shirt. Palmer watched these proceedings with some interest and as Simon leaned across the table to speak, he leaned forward too, for he was piqued by Beckley's strange demeanour.

'I had to leave London,' the thief said in a low voice, wiping his lips with the back of his hand. 'I got work with Squire Penfield up at Wake Manor — have you heard of him?'

'A little,' commented Palmer.

Beckley's eyes shifted about the room and then he beckoned Palmer to draw closer. Dick did so, his face not six inches from the man's cadaverous, pockmarked features. Beckley gulped, took a deep breath and continued: 'He married a Frenchwoman — she was rich. But she's dead now and I know — ' He stopped suddenly and jumped up from his seat.

'What was that?' he cried hoarsely.

'What was what?' enquired Palmer.

'There was a noise outside,' Beckley gasped, his watery eyes widening with fear.

'I think not — I heard nothing,' replied Dick, staring up at him in surprise.

Beckley gripped the edge of the table

nervously. 'Have a look,' he breathed.

Palmer rose, deciding it was best to humour the fellow, and walked over to the window and gazed out. The light from the moon, high amongst the glittering stars, threw long, deep shadows into the corners of the yard, beneath the stable walls and across the cobbles. It was a quiet, peaceful scene.

'Nobody is abroad,' Dick grunted and he returned to his seat.

'You are certain?'

'Of course.'

Beckley sat down again. 'Listen,' he whispered quickly, 'remember what I tell you. He married this French woman many years ago and then he discovered that — ' Beckley reached forward and took a quick drink. 'He discovered that she — '

Suddenly a pistol shot rang out. Beckley gave a shrill cry, clutched his chest and staggered to his feet. He tried to take a step, but instead he slumped forward over the table, upsetting his tankard and spilling the contents over the floor.

Palmer jumped to his feet and gazed down at the man in horror. The ale flowed across the table, turning a dirty, red colour. Without warning Beckley slipped off the edge of the table and fell onto his back. The candle continued to burn in the middle of the pool of blood and ale. Dick Palmer tried to move, but his legs seemed rooted to the floor.

A loud clatter disturbed the silence. Turning, Dick beheld a pistol lying at his feet. He looked up and gazed in a bewildered manner at the open window. His brain was bemused and refused to function properly. He stared down at the pistol again, trying to collect his wits, and at that moment the door opened.

Palmer glanced up and started in amazement. A young woman stood upon the threshold, her hand grasping the door handle tightly. Dick gaped at her, for she was very beautiful. Her black hair, framing a pale, lovely face, fell in soft waves almost to her waist. Dick licked his lips and tried to move, but he could not draw his gaze away from the girl at the door. Her eyes were almost black, and the whole room seemed to be mirrored in their depths.

Suddenly Palmer realised that she was staring at Beckley's body. Her glance moved to the pistol, from the pistol to the open window, and from the window her eyes returned to Dick Palmer standing motionless by the table. As she gazed at him Dick hastened to look elsewhere.

There came the sound of hurrying footsteps in the front of the inn. The girl spoke swiftly in a soft, vibrant voice. 'Quick — come with me!'

She turned abruptly and left the room, glancing over her shoulder to see that he was following. Palmer pulled himself together and stepped quickly across the room. The sound of raised voices and heavy footsteps echoed in the passage. There was not a moment to lose. The girl had opened the door at the end of the passage and Palmer hurried out into the yard, a faint, fragrant perfume filling his nostrils as he passed by her.

He then stopped dead and gasped with surprise. Red Ruby was standing waiting in the yard, saddled and pawing the ground. Holding the reins was the ostler, an expansive grin upon his face. Palmer turned to thank the girl but she waved him away.

'Be gone,' she cried.

Dick hesitated. The sound of the men coming to investigate the shot had grown louder — they were only a few feet away from the corner of the passage. Palmer hesitated no longer, but leapt nimbly into the saddle. Red Ruby rose up onto her hind legs with fright, came down again and, with a shrill whinny, thundered from the yard.

2

The night air fanned Palmer's cheeks as he raced across the green and his heart leaped within him and he bent low and spurred Red Ruby to her utmost.

He left the village at the far side, taking the same road by which he had entered. As he passed into the forest Dick glanced behind and saw a number of men by the inn mounting their horses and preparing to give chase. He flew on between the black, silent trees, the strip of road fading away into the night before him. Red Ruby's hoofs echoed and re-echoed amongst the trees, each echo mingling with the next until the whole forest seemed to be shouting and cheering him on.

Dick Palmer became possessed with the devil, his eyes blazed with excitement and every nerve tingled, every muscle strained and his whole body concentrated on the need for escape. His heart beat a regular tattoo against his ribs — in time with the thud of the horse's hoofs.

Palmer glanced behind again and saw that his pursuers had entered the forest and were not a furlong away. He swept round a sharp corner and then frantically pulled hard on the reins — ahead was another horseman, not twenty yards away. For a second Dick hesitated. But he realised he must go on — that was the only answer. One was better than six. He dug in his spurs again and riding swiftly overhauled the stranger. The latter, riding a big black stallion, suddenly turned in his saddle and stared back at Palmer, then glanced behind Dick at the horsemen in the rear.

Palmer drew level and studied the lone traveller.

He was a huge fellow — a giant of a man. A wild, red beard framed his fierce face.

'Avast!' he roared at Dick Palmer, 'What avails?'

'I am pursued,' rejoined Palmer shortly, and he made as if to ride on.

'Wait!' cried the giant and he turned in

his saddle arid eyed the swiftly approaching villagers. He faced Palmer again.

'Friend,' he cried. 'I can save you!'

'How?'

'I know of a retreat,' replied the stranger and added, noting Palmer's suspicious look. 'It's true, I swear.'

Dick glanced behind at the villagers and then back at the stranger again. 'I can lose nothing by it,' he shouted, 'Lead on.'

'Good,' roared the giant. 'Come — it is a secret place.' He spurred forward and Dick Palmer, having taken another hasty look behind, followed his new friend. They raced swiftly along, Palmer keeping close behind the great bulk of the red-bearded giant. Suddenly the man looked back at Dick.

'Here we take the forest,' he cried.

No sooner said than he pulled his horse hard over and galloped off the highway into the forest. Palmer had no time to consider whether he was taking the right course in following the stranger — events were happening too quickly. The man ahead might be a robber, but he had to take a gamble and he followed the giant, his heart beating like a drum and his nerves tingling with excitement.

The sudden change from riding on the hard road to riding on the soft earth and the consequent silence, was quite startling and Dick for a moment was at a loss, but he soon settled down and concentrated on the skilful horsemanship that was required to manoeuvre between the trees and bushes in the dark. In a few minutes they came out onto a stretch of open ground upon the side of a hill. A stream ran down the middle between steep banks. Dick could hear the water tumbling over the stones and the sound was peaceful and soothing, a welcome change from the last few minutes of tense excitement.

The man in front held up his hand and Palmer pulled Red Ruby to a halt beside him. They had stopped half way down the slope near the edge of the stream and from their positions they were able to watch the highway unseen. The black figures of their pursuers showed up faintly through the trees in the moonlight. The men had halted and obviously were not sure where Palmer and the bearded giant had entered the forest, for they began to ride uncertainly about the fringe of the woods. Their voices floated down to the two horsemen sitting silently on their horses by the edge of the stream.

'The rogues entered here, Harry.'

'No, it was here, Herbert,' answered a deep voice.

Two more voices joined in and the men continued to ride about the road and the edge of the forest, peering at the ground and into the dark woods.

'I can see nothing,' grunted one.

'Perhaps they are nearby, listening to us,' suggested another.

'Or perhaps they are already at the other side of the forest,' cried a third man.

'It's no good,' observed the deep voice despondently, 'they have escaped us — curse their rotten hides!'

'You are right Harry — and it's too dark for further search.'

The villagers appeared disheartened. After further discussion they agreed there was not much hope of tracing the killers

24

now and they pulled their horses around and trotted back to the village. Dick Palmer relaxed and smiled triumphantly to himself in the dark. He felt a touch upon his arm and then a voice boomed in his ear.

'Come, let us eat!'

Palmer stared in surprise at the great bulk beside him. 'Eat?' he queried.

The man nodded and eased his horse to the left and rode off down the valley. Clumps of bushes dotted the slope and Dick's companion made for a large, thick clump about half way down. He rode straight into the bushes, some of which must have been eight feet high, and disappeared. Palmer pulled up abruptly and peered ahead suspiciously, trying to see where the bearded giant had gone. A great roar of laughter burst out from the thicket and echoed about the moonlit valley, mingling with the rush of water between the banks.

'Ride straight on, my friend, it's no trap!'

Reassured, Dick Palmer forced Red Ruby through the bushes, bending low in the saddle to protect his face, and suddenly he found himself in a tiny clearing in front of the narrow opening of a cave. The big thicket covered a steep drop in the side of the sloping valley and the cave was thus hidden from view. The bearded man had dismounted and was tethering his horse to a short pole wedged between two outjuttings of rock. Palmer followed his example.

'I will enter and kindle a light,' quoth the giant. He passed inside and Dick waited, wondering what the cave was like inside. In a few moments a faint glow came from the opening, and Palmer stepped forward and entered.

The cave was large and roomy, as much as fifteen feet long and, Palmer judged, about ten feet wide. The walls were peculiarly ribbed, as if in some bygone age water had lapped their sides. The ceiling was dome-shaped and reached to a point nearly twelve feet above Dick Palmer's head.

A horn lantern stood on a small rock in the centre of the cave and around the latter was strewn a layer of hay. Palmer sat down near the lantern and watched the giant, who was at the back of the cave, preparing a meal. The newcomer, as has been said, was a massive fellow — his great, powerful arms and shoulders and his huge hands seemed almost to fill the cave. His red hair and beard were thick and shaggy, and his blue eyes were set deep and wide in his weather-beaten face.

He came over to Palmer carrying two plates of cold roast chicken. He handed one to the boy and placed the other on the hay and then returned to the back of the cave. Dick Palmer started as he heard the trickle of liquid. The giant came forward again with two brimming tankards of ale and he handed one to Palmer with a large grin on his face.

Palmer gasped. 'This is marvellous!' he cried.

'Yes. I have everything here,' replied the stranger proudly. 'Now let us drink and fill our stomachs — we can talk later.' And without more ado he proceeded to tuck in and Dick Palmer was not slow to follow.

Silence settled in the cave, except for

the sound of crunching jaws. The light from the lantern threw huge, grotesque shadows of the two men on the walls, giving the cave an eerie, ghost-like appearance. Even so there was also a cosy atmosphere about the place that Palmer liked. At last they were finished and Dick's companion lay back on the hay and eyed him speculatively,

'My name is William Snell,' he said. Then he smiled. 'But they call me — Wild Will.'

'Dick Palmer is my name,' replied the boy.

There was a short silence and Palmer realised that Will Snell was waiting to hear his story. Dick therefore settled himself comfortably and began to tell of his adventures up to the time they had first met on the Loughton Road. Will Snell listened in silence to the story and seemed very interested. Now and again he nodded or shook his head, but otherwise he kept quiet, his deep, blue eyes watching Palmer keenly from beneath his shaggy brows. When Dick had finished Wild Will said: 'Ah!' The giant then lay back, staring up at the roof of the cave and smoking his large pipe, which he had produced a little earlier from his coat pocket.

'A strange tale,' he said at last, 'but it doesn't surprise me.'

'How is that?' enquired Palmer.

'I am a gentleman of the road,' said Will Snell grandly. 'By that I mean I move from one occupation to another!' Noting the gleam in Palmer's eyes, he added: 'No — I am not a highwayman — though I admit that that is one of the many excellent professions I have sampled. No,' said Wild Will, 'my last job consisted mainly of evading my excellent friends the customs officials down on the Kentish coast!'

Will Snell lifted his tankard and took a long drink. 'Unfortunately it became necessary that I leave the neighbourhood — things became a little unpleasant,' he remarked. 'I found this cave three or four weeks ago.' He leaned forward then and added mysteriously: 'Some queer things have been going on!'

'What kind of things?' asked Palmer.

'It's not easy to say — I hardly know. Strange happenings — queer rumours in the village, vague and not easy to prove. That's the impression I've gained since I arrived. Now — murder.'

They relapsed into silence, Dick Palmer leaving the question he had specially wanted to ask his new friend until later.

'You will be a hunted man,' commented Will. 'You must discover who the killer is — it's your only chance.'

'Yes — I suppose that is true, but I don't know the district.'

'I will help you.'

'Thank you, my friend. Then tomorrow we must start — but there is one thing that I ought to tell you.'

'And what is that?' asked Wild Will curiously.

'My real name is not Palmer,' said Dick quietly. 'It is Turpin.'

Will Snell's mouth gaped open. 'What!' he cried. 'Blast me timbers — not — ?'

'Yes, I am the son of Dick Turpin.'

'Shake me down,' gasped Will. 'The son of Dick Turpin!'

He stared at Palmer in amazement and then leaned forward and held out his hand. Dick grinned and shook the huge paw that was proferred him. He explained why his mother had changed her name to Palmer.

'A wise move,' commented Will. 'Turpin was not exactly popular with the law of the land — by the way, I believe this was his cave.'

'Aha,' cried Dick delightedly. 'I wondered if it might be.' He stared around at the dim lines of the cave.

'To my best knowledge it is,' said Will. 'He and Bob used to rob travellers on the Loughton Road there which you have just come from, and then they would return here to share the spoils.'

Dick Palmer nodded — all the tales he had heard about his father's wild career now came back to him again.

'Small likelihood it is that Turpin ever thought his own son would frequent his cave,' Will Snell remarked.

'And now I'm not popular with the law,' grinned Dick

'No, but you have an advantage — they

don't know who you are.'

'True,' Palmer said thoughtfully. 'Tell me,' he added with a slight show of embarrassment, 'who is that girl at the inn?'

'Ah,' murmured Wild Will, not without noticing his friend's slight reddening, 'there hangs another strange tale.'

'Why?' enquired Palmer.

'She is the daughter of Harry Murray, Landlord of the Black Horse Inn. Perhaps you recall him. He rarely permits her to leave the inn — she seems to be a prisoner. She is allowed short walks now and again in his company, but it is a strange state of affairs.'

'What's her name?'

'Her name? Oh — I am foolish. Another strange matter — it's French so I believe — Jeanette.'

'Jeanette,' repeated Dick, staring abstractedly at the lantern.

'I do allow,' grinned Will, 'she be a very fine wench.' Suddenly he burst into a roar of laughter.

'Ah, but I like you Dick,' he cried. 'Here you have a murder upon your hands and what do you do? — you think of a girl.' Wild Will gave a long, loud guffaw, his great beard quivering with mirth.

He quieted down again. 'Tomorrow we must make plans,' he said seriously. 'Tonight we sleep.'

'On the morrow I shall seek out Jeanette,' said Dick Palmer.

Wild Will gaped. 'You are mad,' he cried. 'You will be taken and hanged before the day is out.'

'I will take the risk — I must thank her.'

Will Snell glared at him, bent forward and laid a large land on Palmer's knee. He was about to speak but then changed his mind. He stared at his young friend for a second or so and then slowly withdrew his hand, shrugged his shoulders and sat back.

In a few moments Will leaned forward and quenched the lantern and then lay back on the hay and composed himself for slumber. Dick stretched out too, feeling content and at ease. For a long while he stared up at the black roof of the cave, thinking. At last he turned over and fell asleep.

3

Palmer was awakened the following morning by the warm rays of the sun streaming through the bushes into the cave. He sat up and sniffed the air. The pleasant, aromatic smell of fried bacon drifted into the den on the morning breeze.

Dick glanced around him — Will Snell was not there. He jumped to his feet, stretched, yawned and stepped across to the mouth of the cave and looked out into the tiny glade. Wild Will was sitting upon a rock in a shadowy corner before a crackling fire. Around the fire were four blackened stones and upon these was set a frying pan. A number of breakfast delicacies sizzled and spat in the pan, jumping about in a right appetizing manner.

Will Snell glanced up. 'Avast, me boy — top o' the morning to you. Did you sleep well?'

'Excellently, Will. The best sleep I have had this many a day.'

'Good. Come on, the meal is ready. The horses have been seen to, so let us eat.'

Finding another rock by the fire — which Will had procured from the bed of the stream — Dick sat down and took the plate that was proffered him. Will dealt out the succulent fried meats and these imparted an ambrosial perfume so delectable that Dick, directly his plate was full, set to without delay. At this Will was highly pleased and soon followed his young friend's example.

Outside life in the forest was already in full swing. The birds sang gaily and the bees buzzed industriously, but above all was the sound of the tumbling stream as it rushed down the valley. The dew-tipped grass on the slopes glistened in the morning sun and the whole dell was filled with life. The forest formed a dark, green wall around the open ground, its leafy canopy arresting the long shafts of sunlight. But here and there were gaps of bright sunshine where some great tree had fallen.

Dick Palmer felt excited and he ate his breakfast in haste. Will, having contemplated his companion for some while, suddenly got up and went inside the cave. He returned a minute later and handed Palmer a small, marble-handled pistol.

'It is necessary that we should take to the road, Dick,' the giant said. 'We cannot live on the forest alone. You'll find that a good friend.'

Palmer accepted the pistol, but did not answer at first. He had often thought about the game of High Toby and he had often fancied himself as a gentleman of the road. Now that he was face to face with it, however, he felt a little nervous. But this soon passed and the next second his heart was beating excitedly against his ribs.

'Thank you Will,' Dick replied. 'I agree — it's the survival of the fittest these days.' He stuck the pistol in his belt. 'In any case — for me there is no alternative and we may gain news of the killer.'

'Wooing the landlord's daughter will not assist you,' grunted Will, with a grin, as he placed a large piece of meat into his great mouth.

'Ah, but it will. It was at her house the deed was committed, so she may be able to help.'

'Yes, it's a chance,' admitted Will, 'if you remember to broach the subject,' he added meaningly. He wiped his lips appreciatively with the back of his hand.

'The Squire, I warrant, knows more about the matter than he would be willing to admit,' commented Palmer. 'It was of him that Beckley was going to speak.'

'Yes,' agreed Will. 'We must solve the problem by hook or by crook.'

Palmer rose, stretched and patted his stomach. 'I think I will ride round to the back of the inn,' he remarked.

'Yes, that will be safest.'

Palmer strode across to his steed, saddled her and in a few moments was ready for the road.

'Take care,' warned Will, 'all hands be against you.'

Dick Palmer nodded and then with a wave he dug his spur into Red Ruby's flanks, broke through the thicket and cantered away up the dell. Will Snell got to his feet and crossed over to the bushes and watched him go. When Dick had disappeared into the forest he ran across to his own black stallion and began saddling him. In a minute the horse was ready and mounting, Will spurred forward and rode out of the den.

Dick Palmer rode slowly, threading his way through the forest, on the alert for any sign of strange riders. He realised his was a reckless mission but he felt drawn towards the Black Horse Inn.

Red Ruby snorted impatiently and tossed her aristocratic head at the slow pace but Palmer retained a firm grip upon the reigns and at last the mare settled down to a steady trot. Palmer travelled through the forest parallel to the road and, in a little while he came to the edge of High Beach Green. He gazed across the green at the inn, searching the low, brooding place for sign of life but all was quiet and motionless. He pulled Red Ruby to the left, moving deeper into the forest to cross the road, and then began to circle the green a few feet from the edge. He passed by the little church with its square tower and gloomy cemetery surrounded by the dark forest and a few moments later he could see through the trees the stables behind the inn.

Palmer wondered as he dismounted where the ostler was, for that cheerful youth might be of assistance. He tied his mare to a tree in a small green hollow bounded by bushes and then crept forward towards the gap between the stables leading to the yard. He reached the spot safely and glanced swiftly about. The yard was empty and the inn itself seemed lifeless.

What now? Could he risk an open visit to the inn? Dick contemplated the building speculatively but an unexpected solution to the problem was forthcoming.

''Mornin', stranger!'

Palmer spun around at the sound of the voice behind him, his hand flying for his pistol. It was the slim, brown-eyed ostler, a large grin on his face. Dick eyed him suspiciously.

'What do you want?' he asked roughly.

'I think that question belongs to me,'

replied the ostler cheerfully. Palmer grabbed the boy's arm and dragged him behind one of the stables. The ostler remained passive and allowed himself to be pushed hard up against the wall.

'What is your name?' asked Palmer.

'Nicholas Wilken,' replied the boy; then he added confidentially: 'Miss Jeanette calls me 'Naughty Nick'.'

Dick Palmer glared at him. 'Why did you help me to escape?' he snapped.

'Miss Jeanette said you were not the man that killed Simon Beckley!'

Palmer gasped and gazed in astonishment at the ostler. The youth gently disengaged himself from Palmer's grip and leaned nonchalantly against the wall. Dick's thoughts tumbled over one another. How did the woman know this?

'Where is your mistress?' he asked quickly.

'You want to see her?' queried the youth. Dick Palmer nodded impatiently.

The ostler tried to move away but Palmer suddenly grasped his arm again and glared at him suspiciously. 'It had better be no trap,' he growled.

The ostler grinned. 'You can trust me,'

said he. 'I will tell Miss Jeanette you are here.'

Palmer released his arm. 'If you fail me,' he warned, fingering his pistol suggestively, 'it will go sorely with you.'

The ostler was in no wise abashed, however, and he walked away round the corner of the stable whistling a merry tune. Dick Palmer moved back into the forest and waited, his heart beating rapidly. Hours seemed to pass by and he began to wonder if the ostler had failed him and that at this very moment some of the villagers were laying a plan to catch him. Everything was still and a rather ominous silence had settled upon the forest. Once or twice Dick glanced around him apprehensively. He began to sweat with the strain.

Then suddenly there came the sound of quick, light footsteps on the cobbles of the yard. Dick Palmer's heart leaped within him. He drew deeper into the forest, his heart racing like a mad thing. He waited, his eyes glued on the gate between the stables.

Without warning she appeared and

Dick almost stopped breathing. She stood hesitantly in the gap, breathing hard and glancing anxiously about her. Her long black tresses waved gently in the breeze and her dark eyes shone brightly. She had hastened from the inn when Wilken had found her and now her bosom heaved beneath the bodice of her dress. Dick's eyes took in every detail — the high arch to her eyebrows, the long sweep of her lashes and the delicate line of her mouth.

At last Palmer stepped forward out of his hiding place and walked slowly towards her. She gasped at sight of him. He stopped a few paces away.

'Good morning, Miss Murray,' said Palmer, 'and an excellent morning it is to be sure.'

She stared blankly at him for a second or so and then, without replying, she walked quickly past him towards the forest. She reached the edge and turned and beckoned to him to follow. Looking a little surprised, Dick hurried after her and they came to the hollow where Red Ruby was tethered. Here she turned swiftly upon him.

'You fool — are you mad?'

Palmer jumped and reddened like a naughty schoolboy beneath her fierce gaze. Quickly he pulled himself together and straightened his shoulders.

'I come to offer you my grateful thanks, my lady,' said he haughtily, 'for your assistance yesterday in making good my escape from the Black Horse.'

She considered him carefully for a few minutes and then suddenly she sat down upon the bank and indicated that she would like him to do the same. Again a little surprised, Palmer did as she wished, and thereupon a lingering perfume entered his nostrils and he was afraid to look at her. At last he did, however, and they gazed silently at each other.

'What is your name?' she asked at last.

'Dick Palmer. Yours is, I believe, Jeanette Murray?'

She nodded. 'I think you are stupid. Don't you know the squire's head warden, Jack Gregory, is in the inn?'

'May he enjoy his ale,' said Dick cheerfully.

The girl glared at him. She leaned

forward. 'He has been ordered to capture you dead or alive,' she cried heatedly. 'Simon Beckley worked for the Squire.'

'Oh yes,' said Palmer, still not appearing particularly interested but more taken up with studying the girl's beauty. 'Tell me,' he asked, 'why did you help me to escape?'

She laughed lightly. 'Aha! For many reasons. The pistol on the floor — I heard the clatter before I came into the room. The open window and you by the table as if petrified. You had the wrong look on your face. Oh no, you did not kill Simon Beckley.'

Palmer glared wrathfully at her. 'You cannot say that — you have no proof,' he cried hotly. 'I might have been acting.'

She shook her head and smiled. 'No, you were not acting; you didn't kill him. Of that I am certain — more certain, it appears, than you. What do you intend doing?' she added.

'Find out who killed Beckley,' he replied, leaning against the grassy bank and gazing up through the foliage at the blue sky above. 'I shall then force him to admit to the murder or obtain proof by other means.'

'I see,' said she quietly. 'How are you going to live in the meantime?'

Palmer told her his story, of his meeting with Will Snell and their decision to become highwaymen.

She sat up straight at that and was suddenly angry. 'A highwayman?' cried she. 'It's a wicked profession, there is no need for that.'

'We see no other solution,' Dick replied, sitting up too and staring at her in surprise.

She did not answer but turned her head and gazed off into the forest, her little nose and chin held high. Dick's glance fell upon her hand that lay upon the grass near him and he noticed for the first time, upon her second finger, a beautiful gold ring with a fine solitaire set on a deep mounting. The stone flashed brilliantly in the rays of the sun.

'That's a lovely ring you're wearing,' he commented.

'I have had it since I was a child,' she replied shortly, not turning but seeming extremely interested in a robin that was singing cheerily on a far branch.

Dick Palmer decided to try something else. 'Why are you watched so carefully?' he asked suddenly. He saw her start and then frown slightly. She swung round upon him and looked at him anxiously.

'Where did you hear that?' she asked.

'Will Snell.'

She began drawing figures in the dry soil with her slim finger. She said: 'My father fears for me — there are many highwaymen and thieves abroad.'

'I see,' murmured Palmer but he thought she seemed a little hesitant.

Suddenly the girl rose. 'I must go,' she said quietly, dusting her dress.

'Oh!' cried Palmer, unable to conceal his disappointment. 'May I see you again?' he asked.

'If you wish,' she replied. Then she added in a kinder tone: 'But it is dangerous; you must take great care.'

'I will come tomorrow evening.'

Jeanette nodded very slightly and then, gathering up her dress, she ran swiftly away towards the inn. Dick Palmer stood watching her slim figure until she was out of sight. At last he turned and crossed the hollow to Red Ruby. He mounted and was about to ride off when he heard the sound of horse's hooves and the crashing of bushes. Palmer hesitated, not sure which direction to take, but before he had time to reach a decision three horsemen burst from the trees and speedily surrounded him.

'That is he — that is the rogue!' cried one excitedly, a dark, burly fellow with protruding ears. Dick spurred forward, intending to break through, but the man in the centre suddenly produced a pistol.

'Stand, stranger, or I shoot!' The speaker was tall and fair and was smartly dressed in black and he had a commanding air about him.

Dick Palmer knew the fellow meant business and he cursed himself for not thinking of drawing his own weapon. He awaited the next move, watching each man closely. His heart beat rapidly but he felt quite cool and collected. The third man was younger than his companions and Palmer could see that he was highly excited.

'Dismount!' ordered the man in black.

Palmer's brain raced. He well knew once he had dismounted all chance of escape was gone. The man held the pistol steadily. Feverishly Dick tried to think of some way out but there was none — he was well and truly trapped. He began very slowly to dismount.

His foot had already touched the ground when a crashing of bushes disturbed the tense silence. Behind the three men there burst out of the forest a lone horseman, masked and riding a great black stallion. Clenched in his fist was a heavy horsewhip. He charged straight into Palmer's captors and without more ado began laying the whip about him with great energy.

Cries of anguish rang out and the three men tried frantically to escape the stinging thong of the horsewhip as it whistled through the air. The man in black dropped his pistol and pandemonium reigned. The lone rider suddenly spurred forward past the screaming men and, as he reached Palmer, roared out in a mighty voice: 'Follow me!'

Dick Palmer leaped quickly back into the saddle and, pulling Red Ruby about, he galloped after the masked horseman, who was making for the stable yard. Palmer soon caught up with his rescuer and together they thundered across the yard and out on to the road in front of the Black Horse Inn. Behind in the forest, confusion still reigned.

A number of villagers appeared at the door of the inn and stared open-mouthed at the two horsemen. Suddenly one man, a small, thin-faced individual, drew a large pistol from his belt and took careful aim at Dick Palmer as he raced away across the green.

'Look out, Dick!' cried the masked horseman. Palmer swung about in his saddle and saw immediately his danger. He pulled Red Ruby hard over to the right and ducked at the same time, and as he did so a bullet whistled by close to his head. The man on the black stallion, who was some distance away, looked across at Palmer in an anxious manner.

'I'm all right, Will,' cried Dick, grinning. 'He missed!'

'Good,' roared Will in reply.

They bent to their steeds and charged across the green at a tremendous pace, a cloud of dust billowing out behind them. As they entered the forest they glanced back but as yet there appeared no sign of pursuit.

Wild Will gave a triumphant cry: 'Avast! We are away!'

They passed swiftly down the road and in a minute reached the path leading off to the valley. Dick took the lead and they careered along at a reckless pace. In a little while the two men broke out of the trees on to the green slope of the valley and galloped down towards the big thicket. They rushed through the bushes into the glade and dismounted, panting and sweating. They were safe.

They collapsed on the ground and took in great gulps of air. Will removed his mask and turned to his friend.

'Dick, me lad, you will be the death of me!'

Palmer smiled and suddenly broke into loud laughter. 'Ah, Will, how rightly you are called Wild Will. You looked most terrifying and, indeed, it was a desperate move. They nearly took me.'

'Yes, I could see that you were in a sore plight. Pucky is a dangerous customer.'

'Pucky?' queried Dick.

'That was the Chief Constable of Loughton — the fair, red-faced man in black. The other was Robert Mason, the keeper of Epping Forest, and the young fellow was Hatchley, his assistant.'

'Ah, I see,' said Palmer. 'I thought the man in black was a rather cool customer. The Chief Constable of Loughton, eh?'

Will Snell nodded and then he leaned forward thoughtfully towards Dick. 'Do you know who it was that fired at you?' he asked.

There was a silence, for at first Palmer did not reply. Then he said slowly: 'Strange you should ask me that, Will. I feel I have seen him somewhere before.'

'He tried deliberately to kill you; that was no aimless shot.'

'Yes, I admit it did appear so. I wonder — I wonder if it was Jack Gregory.' Palmer glanced quickly at Will to see if the name made any impression but Will's face remained expressionless. 'Jeanette Murray told me,' Dick continued, 'that the Squire's head warden, Jack Gregory was in the Black Horse this morning. She says the Squire has ordered him to capture me dead or alive. Beckley worked for the Squire.'

'Ah-ha, I see what you mean.' Suddenly Palmer slapped the side of his leg. 'I remember,' he cried. 'It was he that sat outside the Black Horse Inn on the night of Beckley's death!'

Will Snell's blue eyes gleamed triumphantly. 'Now we are getting somewhere, my friend; the Squire would not trouble to avenge the death of one of his labourers. Perhaps he is connected with the matter after all — if the man that fired at you was Jack Gregory.'

They sat in silence, each with his own thoughts. At last Dick spoke: 'How do you fancy a visit to Squire Penfield, Will — we might discover something of interest?'

'You mean a secret call — to watch the place and see if anything happens?'

'Yes; no harm can come of it.'

'It's a risky venture but a good idea. We might try it.'

They stared at each other thoughtfully, deliberating upon the suggestion. All at once Will jumped to his feet. 'First, my friend, we must eat. The hour is late; we can plan better on full bellies.' And he strode across the glade into the cave.

4

The afternoon was warm, the sun shining relentlessly down upon the treetops, so that a haze gathered and shimmered over the forest. Life was still and quiet, for the animals and birds rested.

Dick Palmer and Will Snell lay stretched out upon the grass in the little glade outside the dark opening of the cave. They had eaten well. They spoke not but stared up at the blue sky thinking and dreaming. Now and again the quietness was broken by the warning cry of a bird.

Will sat up, filled his pipe and lit it with the glowing end of a stick he withdrew from the fire. He stared into the dying embers and puffed contentedly at his briar.

'I told you not, Will, I think, of the old lady in the cottage,' remarked Dick Palmer.

'No,' replied the giant, still staring into the fire.

Palmer thereupon recounted the incident, telling of the sudden arrival at the cottage of the Squire and two of his men. 'The old woman was relieved to see him,' Dick said.

'Penfield visited old Sally Burke?' cried Will. 'Gibbering gibbets, but that's strange.'

'Who is she?' asked Palmer.

'She was once Louisa Penfield's handmaiden. It isn't like the Squire to visit his sick employees — he's not that considerate.'

'And who is Louisa Penfield?'

'She was the Squire's first wife who died this many a day.'

'Ah, I see,' commented Dick. 'Perhaps the Squire was attached to the old woman?'

'I doubt it — he knows no kind act. What did they speak about?'

'I heard little, they spoke in a whisper.'

'A queer matter,' observed Will, puffing away at his pipe.

Dick Palmer closed his eyes and began to doze. Life in the forest was awakening after the midday rest and the songs of the birds and the cries of the beasts were soon in full chorus.

'We ought to ride to the Squire's house whilst it is still light,' suggested Will. 'Just before dusk is a good time I think.'

'Yes, that is best,' agreed Dick.

'Directly night has fallen they will close up and retreat into the inner precincts and we shall see nothing.'

'After tea, then. I hope the trip is not in vain.'

Will Snell suddenly jumped to his feet and stared anxiously out through the bushes. He held up one hand. 'Listen!' he whispered tensely.

Above the rippling of the brook and the warbling of the blackcaps in the thicket there came the sound of the soft thud of horses' hooves on the forest turf. Dick rose quietly and joined his friend at the edge of the glade and they gazed keenly through the bushes for sight of the intruders. Faint though the sound was it was unmistakable, and the abrupt departure at that moment of the blackcaps towards the south told its own tale.

'Up near the high road,' whispered Will.

They pushed out through the bushes as far as they dare without revealing themselves but a clear view of the road was unobtainable from inside the den. They waited, their eyes anxiously scanning the edge of the forest. Then quite without warning, three men rode out of the trees at the top of the dell and trotted down the slope towards the cave.

'The Chief Constable!' breathed Will Snell.

Dick Palmer turned and hurried into the cave. He reappeared carrying their pistols. Will accepted his and they retreated to the cave mouth, loaded their weapons and waited in silence.

Dick's thoughts tumbled over one another. What if they were discovered? He knew their only hope was to fight; better to be killed here than to die on the scaffold with a wild, jeering mob before you. At this thought his heart beat faster.

The three horsemen drew nearer. 'It's the three I encountered this morning,' Dick whispered. 'Surely they could not have followed us?'

Wild Will shook his head, his blue eyes

glued on the three horsemen not twenty paces away. 'They are here by chance, I'd say,' he replied.

The constable and his men approached the thicket and Palmer compressed his lips and tightened his grip upon his pistol. His nervousness had gone now and he felt cool and grimly determined not to be taken. Will Snell's great jaw jutted forward and he waited, poised like a wild beast.

The horsemen drew level, little knowing that two pistols were trained on their hearts. They were not five paces away from the thicket when suddenly a twig snapped with a loud crack on the far side of the dell. The three men swung round to their left and saw a red squirrel scurry up the trunk of a tree. When they faced the front again they had passed the hidden cave and the two highwaymen had lowered their pistols. Dick sighed with relief. Robert Mason, the keeper of Epping Forest, leaned towards the Chief Constable. 'I swear, sir, it's around these parts they're hid.'

The Constable shrugged his shoulders.

'No doubt, but where?'

Mason did not answer but renewed his keen scrutiny of the surrounding woods.

' 'T'would prove simpler if Thomas Morris was alive,' observed the Constable, as they entered the forest again. 'As you no doubt are aware, he accosted Dick Turpin himself outside the highwayman's retreat; thus he was the only man to discover the notorious rascal's hideout.'

'But Turpin shot him dead,' said Mason.

'He did — the rogue!'

'You think that these scoundrels may have discovered the hideout and are using it for the same purpose?'

'It's a likelihood.'

'More than a likelihood,' grunted Will with a grin. He wiped his forehead as the three horsemen passed out of sight. 'I thought it was all up with us, Dick,' he gasped. 'I could hear the gibbet creaking!'

Dick Palmer sat down upon one of the rocks and loosened his cravat. Will suddenly turned and entered the cave. He appeared again carrying two tankards of ale.

'A fine idea,' cried Dick, jumping to his feet. 'To the Chief Constable of Loughton,' he cried, with a loud laugh. And the two friends drank that worthy's health with enthusiasm.

Wild Will stepped over to the bushes and pushed his way out and gazed down the dell at the spot where the Constable and his men had re-entered the forest. He returned to the den with a strange gleam in his eyes and went into the cave. In a short while he appeared, grinning broadly and carrying two black masks. He handed one to Palmer. Dick looked up at the giant questioningly.

'Let us accost them, Dick,' he cried, 'and demand their valuables.'

Palmer gasped, stared in amazement at his friend and then burst into a roar of laughter. 'And avenge their attack on me this morning,' he cried in delight. 'Ah, but it's a brilliant notion, Will.'

'To the horses, then!' roared the giant.

The two men quickly adjusted their masks, mounted their steeds, broke through the bushes and were, in no time at all, heading in the direction taken by the Constable and his men.

Palmer suddenly slowed down. 'Not so hasty, Will; we dare not rob them near the cave.' Will Snell nodded in agreement and they slowed to an easy canter. They rode on for some minutes, traversing the forest in silence. At last when a good distance from the cave, they broke into a gallop again. The forest here — west of the dell — was comparatively open and the two men were able to make good progress. They scanned the surrounding woods keenly, alert for any sign of their quarry, their hands never far from their pistols. Soon they reckoned they must be pretty near to the three officers and they changed their speed to a cautious trot.

'We should see them any time now,' said Will.

Hardly were the words spoken than, in the distance, they saw the three men they were after sitting their horses in the middle of a glade conversing.

'Ride to the south,' whispered Will, pointing in that direction. 'I'll approach from the north. When you see I have accosted them, make your appearance.'

Dick nodded and they parted, each riding silently towards his objective.

A line of bushes circled the glade and these assisted the robbers. The Constable and his men could be seen over the top of the bushes in the centre in deep conversation quite unaware of their danger. Dick reached his position south of the glade without being seen and from a vantage point he watched the far side expectantly. The three men had drawn their horses together in a circle and their backs were to the trees.

Suddenly Wild Will burst out of the forest and Dick himself started in surprise at his friend's abrupt appearance. The giant bore down upon the Constable with great rapidity and his general aspect was so terrifying that Palmer stared at him open-mouthed. The horses of the three men shied with fright and the riders jerked about in their saddles and gazed in consternation upon the intruder. Will Snell did indeed make a fearsome picture with his wild red hair and beard waving in the wind and his blue eyes glittering devilishly behind his mask.

Holding his pistol out in front of him he thundered up to the Constable and slithered to a halt not four paces away. The three officers were quite disconcerted. Upon seeing Will's pistol Dick Palmer realised he had not drawn his own. Quickly he did so and then spurred forward into the clearing.

'Avast, strangers!' roared Will Snell. 'Hand me your valuables.'

Palmer pulled Red Ruby to a halt before the three men and they swung round in their saddles and gazed at him in dismay. He pointed his pistol deliberately at the heart of Robert Mason. That worthy gave a choking gasp and glanced fearfully back and forth at the two robbers.

The Chief Constable, however, sat calmly upon his steed and stared at the highwaymen speculatively. Young John Hatchley, his eyes bulging from his head, raised his arms high above his head.

'Withdraw your weapons and hand them to me,' cried Will.

The three men obediently did as they were ordered, the Constable holding his back to the last. Will Snell watched him warily for he knew Pucky would snatch at the slightest chance to turn the tables on them. But, very slowly, the Chief Constable handed over his weapon. Will relaxed a little and Palmer saw him smile beneath his mask.

'Friend robber,' he called to Dick, 'relieve these gentlemen of their valuables.'

Palmer leaned forward and cheerfully collected the many pieces of silver that the officers pulled reluctantly and in silence from their pockets. Will Snell, meanwhile, continued to cover them with his pistol, fearing that one of them might suddenly produce a concealed weapon.

'Thank you,' said Palmer mockingly, when he had collected all that they handed him. 'You are sure you own nothing further?'

'Who are you, villains?' cried the Constable, abruptly losing his composure.

Will Snell laughed derisively and then, waving his arm at Dick, he pulled his horse about and galloped back into the forest.

Palmer, depositing their ill-gotten gains in his pockets, spurred past Pucky and his men, waving to them jauntily, and followed hard on his friend's heels. The three robbed men did not move but gazed after them with impotent rage.

The highwaymen raced away through the trees and made a wide detour to the north before turning and heading back towards the hideout. Their caution proved unnecessary, however. The Constable did not follow — he obviously considered it foolish to trail the robbers through the forest unarmed.

About an hour later Will and Dick sat before the mouth of the cave greedily swallowing large portions of cold roast beef. The afternoon's escapade had given them a fine appetite. On the way back Dick Palmer had counted their spoils and they had enough, as Will commented, to feed themselves well for the next three months.

'We'll rest for a while,' suggested the giant, 'and then repair to the manor.'

'We must take care,' Palmer observed. 'It will be common knowledge the

Constable has been robbed and the countryside will be alive with people looking for us.'

'You are right; the journey may be dangerous but you are a fully fledged highwayman now, so why worry?'

They rested. Dick Palmer thought of the second visit he intended making later that evening when darkness had fallen to the Black Horse Inn. He felt content and the fact that he was a hunted man did not seem to bother him.

The sun set and the brightness of the afternoon faded and was soon replaced by the grey mantle of early evening. The forest became quiet and a serene peacefulness reigned over everything.

'I think the hour is ripe,' exclaimed Dick

Wild Will nodded and the two rose to their feet and untied their horses. Red Ruby and the black stallion had received a rub down following the afternoon's exercise and, being well fed and rested, they now whinnied with pleasure as their masters prepared them for the road.

Will led the way up the slope of the dell

towards the highway, trotting quietly over the grass. They had agreed to speak as little as possible, for silence and stealth were required on such an expedition as this. Upon reaching the Loughton road they made sure there were no villagers abroad and then they spurred along towards High Beach.

At a certain point some four hundred yards from the village the Loughton road joined the Epping road, and it was here that Will Snell turned north on to the latter highway and they rode forward to Wake Manor. In a quarter of an hour Dick's companion broke off left into the forest. They now moved slowly, making little noise. Suddenly Palmer saw that Will had halted and, upon reaching the giant's side, he found they were on the edge of a private drive.

'Is this it?' whispered Dick.

Will nodded.

The drive opened out further on, circled a big lawn and ended before a grey, sombre house — Wake Manor, the home of Adam Penfield, the Squire of High Beach. Ivy clothed the black stones of the house, surrounding the windows running along the eaves. It was a square, rather squat building and the large, flat, vacant windows stared sightlessly out over the lawn. The great double doors were flanked by two black pilasters and the steps between them seemed small and insignificant in comparison.

Dick Palmer and Will Snell dismounted. On the south side, nearest to them, the forest reached to within a few feet of the house. The gardens and park stretched away on the north side.

'Not exactly a cheerful place,' commented Dick.

Wild Will did not answer — he was watching the house intently.

Great banks of black clouds had now gathered overhead and darkened the evening landscape, and because of this a light was shining from a front room on the ground floor of the manor. This room was quite near the two men hidden in the forest. As they watched there came the sudden sound of a horse's hooves upon the drive. The two men hastily withdrew behind a large tree. In a minute there appeared a man riding at a swift gallop. He passed close by and raced up to the front of the manor.

'It's the man who shot at you, Dick!' hissed Will.

'So it is,' breathed Palmer. 'Jack Gregory, the Squire's head warden.'

The little, sharp-faced man leaped from his horse and ran up the steps of the Manor. He knocked loudly on the big door. In a few minutes a lackey appeared and without a word Gregory hurried inside.

Some time passed by and no sound came from the house. Then, without warning, a horseman rode forward slowly from the back of the building and dismounted at the side of Gregory's horse. The newcomer was a large, thick-set fellow and unpleasant to look upon. In a short time the doors of the Manor opened again and Gregory appeared, seeming like a dwarf between the towering pilasters. The two men nodded to each other and mounted, pulled their steeds around and galloped off at a fast pace down the drive. They reached the high road and gradually the sound of their horses' hoofs faded away into the night, and all that remained was a deep silence and the light burning in the window of the Manor.

'What's going on?' muttered Palmer.

'I don't know,' grunted his companion, 'but I don't like the smell of it.'

'It's a mysterious place,' murmured Dick.

'Let's move nearer to the window,' suggested Will, 'and view the occupants.'

They crept stealthily through the trees and approached the lighted window. Stationing themselves on the very edge of the forest they gazed curiously into the room. There were two occupants. One was the Squire himself. Adam Penfield was a tall man and he was dressed immaculately in a red and grey coat and waistcoat, elegantly embroidered with blue silk. A black wig adorned his smooth, dark features.

The other occupant, Will intimated in Dick's ear, was Charlotte Penfield, the Squire's wife. She was reclining on a long settee by the hearth. She was dressed very elaborately and her petticoat and over-gown were spread out on each side of her over the settee. Her grey overgown opened in the front, as was the fashion of the day, displaying her richly embroidered petticoat. The woman's fair hair was arranged in powdered waves reaching high above her head and her face was heavily painted, seeming like a mask. A large brown patch or beauty spot adorned her left cheek.

Adam Penfield was striding back and forth across the room and his wife watched him in silence, her eyes shining, her lips parted.

'At last they are within our grasp, Charlotte,' cried the Squire. 'It has been a long time. With possession of the certificate, Frickington can go ahead.'

Penfield stopped and faced his wife. 'She will then have no proof — nobody can, with it gone! Ours, my dear, ours!' he cried exultantly. 'God knows I have tried hard and long enough for it.'

Wild Will fingered his black beard and turned to Dick. 'What's the matter with him?' he murmured.

'It's a foolish way to carry on. I don't know what he's talking about.'

'Nor I,' grunted Will.

Suddenly the wild baying of wolf-hounds split the silence of the night air. The two men swung round, fear in their eyes and gazed over towards the far side of the house.

Dick gasped. 'Look!' he breathed.

Bounding across the lawn towards the hidden men were two great wolfhounds. Adam Penfield had also heard the sounds and now he stepped swiftly over to the window.

'Quick — the horses,' cried Will, and without more ado the two men turned tail and raced back through the trees towards Red Ruby and the black stallion. At their movement the hounds gave a terrible, blood-curdling howl and shot forward and broke into the trees not thirty paces behind. Panic lent wings to the two highwaymen and they flew through woods.

If they could only reach and mount their steeds, they would be safe. They burst out into the small glade where the horses were tethered, vaulted into the saddles and plunged in their spurs. The two horses shied with fright, but next moment they crashed forward through the forest at a wild rate, the hounds at their heels. The highwaymen reached the high road and nearly overran into the forest upon the other side, such was their speed. Both men knew what kind of death they could expect at the hands of a wolfhound, and so they didn't spare their horses. Bending well forward in their saddles, they thundered off down the old Epping Road. The hounds soon were left far behind and, seeing their quarry escape, the two beasts halted in the middle of the road and howled dismally.

Dick and Will laughed back at them in derision — and with relief — and they slowed down to a canter. After a little while, when they had regained their breath, they began discussing the strange words they had heard spoken by the Squire.

'I presume — from what we heard the Squire say,' observed Dick thoughtfully, gazing down at the dark road ahead, for night had fallen, ' — that he wishes to obtain some paper — some certificate

— and with it he hopes to receive something of value.'

Will Snell nodded, looking keenly across at his friend, whose pale face he could just make out against the black trees. 'Apparently,' Palmer went on, 'he has done a number of things already to achieve his objective — I'll wager they are of a nefarious character.'

'Without doubt,' said Will.

'We must discover what it is he has done,' Dick remarked, 'and what he intends to do — and why!'

'Good,' grunted Will, 'but it won't be easy.'

'We can but try.'

At this moment they reached the junction with the Loughton Road. To the left lay High Beach, to the right, the cave. Will Snell turned questioningly towards Palmer.

'I will ride on to the inn,' Dick murmured, somewhat sheepishly.

'Good luck, then,' cried Will. 'Watch out for the Constable.'

'That I will,' replied Dick, and he swung his horse to the left and galloped off towards the village. Will watched him go with a slight frown creasing his forehead, then he shrugged his broad shoulders and cantered off towards the cave.

5

The façade of the Black Horse Inn was dark and small, dotted with little white windows and topped by low hanging eaves. The front was misleading, however, for the Inn was a large abode, honeycombed with tiny passages and tiny, inconspicuous rooms. The yellow lanterns, that hung in all manner of places, did but to lighten some parts and darken others.

In the outer wall at the corner in the passage leading to the rear of the house, was a small door, which Dick Palmer had not perceived on his first visit to the Black Horse Inn. This door opened out into another passage, which led to the landlord's living quarters.

A number of doors along this passage opened out into various rooms and these included the back of the bar — on the one side — and a parlour and a kitchen, which faced out over the stable yard

— on the other. In the latter two rooms the Murray family spent much of their time. At the end of the passage on the left, a narrow, steep staircase led to the bedrooms. Opposite the bottom of the stairs there was a small, neat sitting room. This was reserved for special visitors.

On the night with which we are dealing and at a time when Will Snell and Dick Palmer were setting out for Wake Manor as already recounted, Jeanette Murray was seated upon a stool by the parlour hearth bent over some needlework. Harry Murray lolled in an armchair opposite his daughter and Emily, his wife, was preparing a plum pudding in the kitchen.

The landlord of the Black Horse Inn was smoking his pipe, the smoke curled lazily up to the white ceiling. He sat staring thoughtfully into the fire, now and again lifting his head and staring across at Jeanette, as if assuring himself she was still there.

Jeanette, for her part, sat quietly upon the stool, her head bent over her work, part of her long black hair falling down over her bosom. The girl had bathed herself and now was warming her limbs by the crackling wood fire.

Harry Murray looked up at his daughter again. 'Do you fancy a stroll before the inn opens, girl?' he asked.

She glanced up from her work and hesitated before she answered. 'Perhaps — perhaps just a short distance, father,' she replied. She looked at the clock on the mantelpiece. 'Yes for a few moments, if you wish.'

'Come then, don your cloak.'

Jeanette rose, laid her work upon the stone seat in the earth and crossed the room to a large cupboard by the kitchen door. She opened it and withdrew her cardinal — a long, red, hooded cloak — and put it on. They stepped into the kitchen, and crossed over to the door leading into the stable yard. Emily Murray looked up and gazed at them in an anxious manner.

'You are going out?' she queried.

'Yes, for a short while,' replied Harry.

His wife frowned. 'Be careful,' she said.

'Of course, woman.'

The landlord shepherded his daughter

outside and they turned the corner of the inn and passed out onto the green. Around them the village lay quiet and peaceful, patiently awaiting the fall of darkness. They strolled along towards the Loughton Road. On the way the couple passed by a number of villagers and the landlord greeted them cordially. A little further on they turned into the Loughton Road and soon the forest closed in around them.

They spoke little to each other, content to listen to the evening sounds that floated out from the trees on the soft breeze. The forest here, to the south of the village, was broken in parts and now and again pleasant vistas opened out before them. But in between the trees and bushes grew thick and tall, and at these points there was little light upon the road for the foliage almost bridged the narrow track.

Jeanette was very quiet, staring down at the highroad, deep in thought. When she was like this Harry Murray too became quiet, fearing to interrupt her, for, if the truth be known, the landlord held his lovely daughter a little in awe. They carried on along the road, walking slowly and leisurely, the sound of their steps upon the hard surface echoing amongst the trees. Soon they came to the little cottage set back from the highway wherein lived Sally Burke.

'Sally, I hear, is recovering from her sickness,' Jeanette remarked.

Her father nodded, but made no comment.

They passed by and began descending a hill in a deep part of the forest. Harry Murray clasped his daughter's arm tighter and glanced about the fringe of the forest in a rather anxious manner. Black clouds were gathering in the skies now and the light began to fade. Beneath the thick canopy of leaves it became quite dark. Then, without warning, it started to rain.

Harry Murray glanced up at the leaves as a large drop fell on his forehead. Jeanette pulled her hood further over her head. 'We had best return,' she said.

'Yes,' agreed the landlord, 'we are in for a bad night.'

They turned round and were just about

to commence the journey back when a sharp sound from the forest made them halt in their tracks. Harry Murray pushed Jeanette behind him and peered forward into the darkness, reaching for his pistol at the same time.

'Don't touch your weapon,' came a cry from the forest.

Two masked horsemen suddenly rode out of the trees and confronted the couple. One, the smaller of the two, levelled his pistol at Murray. The landlord cursed and kept on drawing his own weapon.

'Take him, Stephen,' hissed the little man.

The second robber, a burly fellow, leaped swiftly from his horse, sprang forward and dealt the landlord a heavy blow across his face. Harry Murray staggered back and all but fell to the ground. Steadying himself, however, he jumped forward again and attacked his aggressor with great fury. Jeanette retreated and stood with her back to a tree-trunk, watching the fight with wide, frightened eyes.

The little man swore profusely and hurriedly dismounted and, ignoring the two combatants, hastened towards Jeanette Murray. The girl gave a low cry of fear and shrank back against the tree. Harry Murray turned at his daughter's cry and the burly robber, taking advantage of the moment, hit him hard in the back of the neck with his great fist. The landlord took one hesitant step forward, then fell heavily to the ground. The little man reached Jeanette and grasped her right arm tightly and wrenched it forward. He gazed down at her fingers, but apparently seeing not what he wanted, he grabbed her other hand. Again he scrutinized her fingers, but he was not satisfied. He glared up into her face and twisted her arm cruelly behind her back.

'Your ring, your ring,' he cried. 'Where is your ring?'

'My ring?' gasped she, sobbing with pain. 'I don't know what you mean.'

'The ring, the ring,' he reiterated. 'The one worn by you.'

'Oh,' Jeanette murmured, suddenly understanding. She glanced down in surprise at her right hand. But just at that moment there came a diversion, for the thud of hoofs was heard in the distance. The little man swung round, as did his accomplice. The landlord, who lay helpless upon the ground, as a result of the diversion, escaped a brutal kick in the face, which the burly robber was about to deliver.

Down through the tunnel of leaves a hundred yards away, silhouetted against the grey light at the end, rode a single horseman, his cloak billowing out behind him. Such was his tremendous pace as he thundered towards the little group, the robbers stared at the newcomer in amazement.

⋆   ⋆   ⋆

After leaving Will Snell at the road junction, Dick Palmer had ridden towards the village and then cut off into the forest. He circled the green, as he had done the previous day, and arrived presently at the back of the Black Horse Inn.

He dismounted, crept up to the stables

and looked about warily. It was his intention to find the ostler, Nicholas Wilken. There was a window high up in the back of one of the outhouses — by standing on his toes Palmer was able to see into the building. The ostler was sitting on a box in a corner of a small loft, polishing a saddle. It was a tiny place, barely furnished and untidy. In another corner was an old bedstead.

Palmer tapped lightly on the pane. The boy looked up with a start and, at sight of the highwayman, his eyes lighted up. Dick beckoned to him and the ostler rose quietly and opened the window.

'Evening to you, stranger,' he greeted.

'Where is Miss Murray?' Palmer asked quickly.

The ostler grinned momentarily. 'She has taken a walk with my master,' he replied.

'A walk?' queried Palmer, and for some unaccountable reason a cold chill ran through him. 'Where — where?' he cried.

Wilken stared down in surprise at the highwayman. 'I heard my master say they would take the Loughton Road.'

Without another word Dick Palmer stepped back from the window and raced away towards Red Ruby.

'What goes on?' shouted the ostler.

But Palmer had no time to explain and, leaping into the saddle, he pulled Red Ruby about, plunged in his spurs, and galloped forward across the stable yard. He broke out onto the road circling the green, and the clatter of Red Ruby's hoofs echoed about the old cottages, but Palmer had entered the Leighton Road before any curious villagers had time to step to their windows and peer out.

A terrible feeling of apprehension had come over the highwayman and cold fingers clutched at his heart, so that he rode Red Ruby as if pursued by the devil. They swept down the road at a breathtaking pace, the steed's hoofs seeming hardly to touch the ground. Palmer's eyes now blazed with a wild light and his lips were set in a grim line as he spurred Red Ruby to her utmost.

In a short while he made out two horses some distance ahead, standing motionless in the rain by the side of the road. He raced on, not slackening speed one whit, his eyes glued to the little group of people that he could now see by the edge of the forest. Soon he picked out Jeanette's red cloak and his heart pounded against his ribs.

When he was about ten paces from them he began pulling on the reins with all his might, but it was of no avail, his speed was too great — he could not halt in time. He thought quickly and as he drew level he recklessly abandoned the reins and threw himself sideways straight at the little robber, who was standing staring at him with open mouth.

He crashed down onto the fellow and a scream of pain rang out as they tumbled to the ground. Dick felt a hard knock upon his knee and for a moment his leg went numb. He glanced down at the man spreadeagled beneath him — the robber lay quite motionless. Palmer scrambled to his feet and out of the corner of his eye he saw the landlord sitting dazed on the grass verge. The second robber was moving towards him.

'Dick!'

It was a soft call from the girl and at the sound of it Palmer thrilled, and hurled himself like a madman at the burly robber. The latter was taken unawares and before he could shield himself Dick Palmer had dealt him a tremendous blow upon the side of the head. The burly fellow stumbled and fell to the ground.

A noise behind him made Palmer turn swiftly, but too late, the small man had risen and was already half way to his horse. Palmer drew his knife and threw it straight at the man's back, but the robber had seen the action and he leaped aside. The knife plunged into the trunk of a tree not a foot away. The fellow gave Palmer a terrified look, scrambled into the saddle, dug in his spurs and galloped off down the road towards Loughton. Dick swung about in time to see the second robber also hurrying to his steed.

'Hold the villain,' he cried to the landlord, but Harry Murray was too weak to be of any assistance.

Palmer jumped after him, but the burly fellow gained his mount. As Dick approached, he lifted his heavy boot and kicked out viciously. The blow caught the highwayman in the chest and he spun round like a top and then collapsed on the ground. In a minute the robber was thundering down the road after his accomplice.

The highwayman regained his feet and looked around for Red Ruby. The mare was some thirty feet away cropping the grass at the edge of the forest.

Jeanette Murray hurried to her father's assistance. 'Do not trouble yourself,' she called to Palmer. 'We are safe now.'

The landlord got slowly to his feet and, leaning on his daughter's arm, hobbled across to the highwayman who was standing in the middle of the road watching, with exasperation, the robbers as they galloped away. They soon vanished into the darkness and all that remained was the echo of their horses' hoofs.

'Stranger,' gasped the landlord weakly. 'This deed of yours I will ever remember. I thank you most gratefully for rescuing us from the scoundrels.'

'It's nothing,' replied Dick.

Harry Murray held out his hand and

the two men shook warmly. 'Who are you?' asked the landlord.

Jeanette, seeing Palmer's hesitancy, turned to her father and exclaimed: 'This is the man they accuse of murdering Simon Beckley!'

Harry Murray jerked up his head and gazed in surprise at Dick Palmer. There was a long silence.

'It cannot be,' growled the landlord at last.

'You speak correctly, sir,' replied the highwayman. 'I was with the fellow at the time, I admit. The pistol, though, was thrown through the window at my feet after the deed was committed.'

The landlord stared at Dick Palmer doubtfully and then he began scratching his woolly, black hair. The three stood in the middle of the dark highway facing each other hesitantly. Quite abruptly the clouds parted and the moon shone through and bathed the group in light. It stopped raining. Harry Murray stared closer at Palmer, noting his youthful appearance.

'It's a strange thing you say,' he

murmured, and again there was silence.

Slowly a smile creased the landlord's countenance. 'Even so,' he said, 'you cannot perform such a deed as this one and commit murder to boot.'

Jeanette gave an audible sigh of relief, but it was cut short as she beheld the painful expression on her father's face. The landlord was sorely hurt.

'Come, let us hasten to the inn,' she cried.

Palmer turned round and gave a soft whistle. Red Ruby, cropping the grass at the side of the road, lifted her head immediately and then came trotting up to her master. Dick helped the landlord to mount, took the reins and, with Jeanette supporting her father as best she could, led the mare slowly back along the road towards High Beach.

'There is a path here that leads round to the back of the Inn,' the girl called to Palmer, pointing to the right. 'Perhaps it would be better if we take it.'

Seeing the narrow track she indicated just ahead, Dick nodded and guided Red Ruby into it.

'What did the rogues want?' asked the landlord of Jeanette, as they traversed the narrow path.

'It was strange,' replied the girl. 'He wanted my ring.'

'Your ring?' queried Dick.

'Yes — I do not understand. It's not of great value.'

'He took it, then?' asked Harry Murray.

'Oh no, he did not. I was not wearing it — I forgot to put it on after my bath!'

Dick Palmer burst into a roar of laughter. 'Then they obtained nothing?' he cried.

'Nothing at all.'

'You were lucky. But it is strange — why should they want your ring?'

They discussed this question together for the rest of the journey, but when they at last arrived at the back of the Black Horse Inn they still had found no satisfactory solution. The ostler appeared in the yard and without a word assisted Palmer to lift the landlord off the horse. Jeanette turned to the youth and whispered something in his ear. Wilken touched his cap and then led Red Ruby off to the stables.

Dick Palmer helped Harry across to the door of the kitchen. Jeanette swung it open and they went inside. Emily Murray was by the kitchen range when they entered. She turned and stared at them, her wrinkled hands flew to her lips and her face grew pale at sight of her husband.

'Harry!' she whispered, in a horrified tone.

In the light from the lamp everyone could now see the landlord's badly gashed features.

6

Emily Murray ran forward and placed an arm round her husband's waist. Her soft, wrinkled face was filled with anxiety and pity. Without a word she led him out into the passage and upstairs.

In the kitchen Dick Palmer stood about awkwardly. At last he turned and looked at Jeanette, who had discarded her cloak and was warming herself by the fire. Then suddenly he noticed a long, red scratch just above the bodice of the girl's dress and his blood ran cold. Involuntarily he clenched his fists, and he strode across to her side and gazed down closely at the scratch. The flesh was quite badly torn and the skin around was inflamed.

'You're hurt,' cried Dick.

She glanced up and smiled. 'It's nothing — it does not pain me.'

'How did it occur?' asked Palmer heatedly, his whole frame quivering with rage at the thought that someone had harmed her delicate skin.

Jeanette rose slowly and, placing her slim hands one on each shoulder, she gazed deep into his eyes.

'Dick, I repeat,' said she, 'it doesn't hurt. Please do not be angry because of it.'

Palmer relaxed, but a cold glint remained in his eyes that did not escape the girl. 'You are a foolish man,' she whispered, her lips reaching up to his. Dick Palmer gathered her in his arms and embraced her.

Emily Murray was heard descending the stairs and in a moment she appeared in the doorway. She stared across the room at Palmer and then slowly she advanced towards the highwayman and stopped just before him. She looked up at him and their eyes met. Emily placed her hand on Dick's big shoulder.

'My son,' she said quietly, 'I know not how to thank you for saving my husband and daughter this evening. It was a brave act.' Emily then rose up on her toes and gently pressed her lips against Palmer's cheek. Dick shuffled his feet and looked embarrassed.

'My husband has told me,' she added, 'your account of the murder. I believe you, too.'

Palmer's feelings were somewhat mixed, but upon hearing her last words he smiled gratefully. All at once he took Emily's hand in his and bowed over it and gently kissed her fingers. 'Thank you, madam,' he said, 'for your trust in me.'

Jeanette had watched this little scene with delight, but now she hurried forward and cried: 'How is father?'

'He will be well,' replied Emily. 'I have bathed and bandaged his wounds and will send for the doctor.' She then turned to Palmer. 'He wishes to speak with you. Will you come?'

Dick nodded, and the three of them crossed the room and passed upstairs. Emily opened the second door on the left along the narrow passage on the floor above, and ushered Palmer inside.

Harry Murray sat propped up against a pillow in a large bed near a small window that looked out over the stable yard. 'Come in, come in,' he cried.

Emily and Jeanette sat down at each

side of the bed and Palmer stood at the foot of the bed. The landlord stared at Dick for some time and then he glanced at his wife. Emily in turn stared at Palmer.

At last she exclaimed: 'It was lucky you were in the neighbourhood tonight.'

'Yes,' Dick murmured and then he suddenly realised they were waiting for him to give an account of himself. Immediately he launched into his story and told them what had befallen him since first he left London. The three of them listened in silence throughout — Jeanette with her head bowed listening intently, for the second time, to his narrative; Emily and Harry staring straight at him. When he had finished the landlord nodded thoughtfully, and then glanced questioningly at his wife. Palmer could see that they all believed him, but they appeared to be wondering whether to tell him something in return. Emily glanced up at Palmer, a strange, hesitating look upon her face.

The highwayman suddenly felt sorry for the little family. It dawned upon him that something worried them, that their lives were marred by some great trouble, and all at once he was curious to know what it was. He saw that they were in two minds on whether to tell him or not.

'What troubles you all?' he asked softly.

Emily started and then smiled wearily. 'Is it so obvious?' she asked.

'I am afraid it is.'

An awkward silence settled upon the group. Suddenly Jeanette jumped to her feet and gazed earnestly at her parents. 'Tell him, please tell him,' she cried. 'We cannot always remain like this, in daily terror!'

Harry and Emily Murray stared worriedly at each other. At last the landlord nodded his head. 'Tell him woman. It can do no harm.'

Emily turned slowly and faced the highwayman, a tired expression in her pale, blue eyes. 'What I tell you now, my son,' she said, 'has never before been told to man nor woman.'

Jeanette sat down again and lowered her head, and her long hair fell down over her bosom and hid the scratch. Harry

Murray leaned forward, staring blankly before him, and Emily rested her head against the wall and clasped her hands in her lap.

'I like the look of you, Dick, that is why I tell you now. Perhaps you may be able to help us. Firstly,' and now Emily drew a deep breath, 'Jeanette is not our daughter.'

Dick Palmer raised an eyebrow, but otherwise remained expressionless, saying no word.

Emily went on: 'We found her in a basket in the forest when she was about two years old. In a little casket, which was tied around her waist next to her skin, was a note with one word written on it — 'Jeanette'. The note itself was wrapped around that ring she now wears.'

Emily Murray raised a quivering hand to her lips and fingered them nervously. Her husband kept quite still, staring with an almost vacant look across to the far side of the room.

'We had no children of our own so — we adopted her. We told no one. We had been away from the village for a few years and we returned — with a baby. It appeared quite natural to the villagers and they suspected nothing.'

Dick glanced at Jeanette. She was sitting quietly on her chair, staring across at Emily Murray.

'When Jeanette was six,' Emily continued, 'some thieves entered her room. They upset all her drawers, the tables and cupboards, then escaped, taking nothing.'

The woman paused and leaned forward, staring intently at Palmer. 'Since that day,' she said, 'the house has been searched many times, but every time they seemed not to have found what they wanted.'

Emily sat up straight and raised one hand. 'That is not all. I believe it is four times now Jeanette herself has been molested when abroad — and once in the inn, when Harry was down in Loughton.'

Dick Palmer was intrigued by the story. 'But have you never seen the rascals?' he cried.

'Never — when they have attacked Jeanette they have been always masked.'

'What do they seek?'

'We don't know.'

'Do you wonder,' said the landlord suddenly, 'that we fear for her safety?'

'The Chief Constable knows nothing of this?'

'We dare not mention the matter to him,' Emily replied, 'for we fear we might lose Jeanette as a consequence.' The woman then shook her head slowly, indicating that this they could not bear.

Dick nodded understandingly and silence settled down on the room. The highwayman stared thoughtfully out of the window, and the little family gazed at him anxiously, wondering what he would do.

At last Palmer stepped back from the end of the bed. He looked at Jeanette and again he noted the scratch that spoiled her soft flesh and he became angry. She gazed back at him and frowned, for she saw how he felt.

Dick glanced from one to the other, feeling now rather important. 'If it is within my power to help you,' he said earnestly, 'I will with all my energy.' Then he swung around abruptly and strode to the door.

'What will you do about Simon Beckley?' Emily called.

All three of them watched Palmer keenly as they waited for his answer. The highwayman stopped with his hand upon the door knob. He turned round and faced them.

'I think,' he replied quietly, 'that the two matters will solve each other!'

A dead silence followed this statement, and then Palmer opened the door and stepped out into the passage, feeling highly satisfied with the effect his last words had had on the family.

'I'll accompany you downstairs,' Jeanette called and, at a nod from her mother, she hurried after the highwayman. They descended the stairs together and Jeanette led the way into the parlour.

'Remain here,' she said, 'I will make you a cup of tea before you leave.' Palmer seated himself, glad to relax for a few moments after his hard ride. Jeanette soon returned and handed him a steaming cup of hot tea. She then squatted before him and watched him sip the liquid.

When he had finished Jeanette said: 'It is late and time my mother opened the inn.'

Palmer grunted. 'True — and time I suppose I was away.' They gazed upon one another a little longer and then Jeanette led the way into the kitchen and opened the back door. 'Take care,' she whispered.

Palmer nodded and without looking at her again he stepped out into the yard. He waited until the door had closed quietly behind him and then strode towards the stables. Nicholas Wilken was standing by the stable door, a large grin upon his face and a merry twinkle in his big, brown eyes.

'My steed!' growled Dick Palmer.

The boy's smile vanished and he obediently hurried into the stables. In a few moments he reappeared leading Red Ruby, saddled and looking well refreshed. Palmer noted her clean, fresh appearance.

'You are an ostler after my own heart,' he grunted.

The highwayman mounted immediately and, nodding at Wilken, rode quietly out of the yard. A number of villagers were waiting impatiently outside the front of the inn, some of them gazing in through the windows to see if they could see any signs of life. They took little heed of the lone horseman that passed by and Palmer was soon away across the green.

It was a fine night, for all the clouds had rolled away and the moon and stars shone brightly. The western sky was fringed with a pale, opalescent glow, lending to the firmament a strange, supernatural appearance. The village lay quiet and still, the lights from the tiny windows twinkling cheerfully, as they had done on the night Dick Palmer had first entered High Beach. He reached the Loughton Road and restrained Red Ruby to an easy canter, for he wished to think.

Upon one thing Palmer felt certain. The two men he and Will Snell had seen ride away from the Squire's house and the two men who had attacked the landlord and his daughter that evening, were one and the same. What was the Squire's game, the highwayman wondered.

7

At the fork Dick Palmer turned right towards Wake Manor, riding slowly and staring down thoughtfully at the bobbing head of Red Ruby. It began to dawn upon the highwayman that the apparently disconnected incidents that had occurred lately in High Beach had, in actual fact, all been deliberately arranged and were part of some strange, recondite plan.

But what was the purpose of it all? Dick scratched his head and dug in his spurs for the chestnut mare had slowed almost to a halt. The dark silence of the forest was congenial to thought and Palmer was glad of the chance it gave him to study the mystery that revolved around the village of High Beach.

The highwayman glanced up after several minutes riding and realised that he was not far from Wake Manor. He remembered now that Will Snell once told him there was an inn farther down the road. It would be better that he planned his next move over a quart of ale. He rode on past the Manor and in a little while came to a lonely inn nestling well back in the forest.

'Jack's Retreat' — for such was the name of the inn — was a very small place, but lamps shone cheerfully from the little windows and bathed the old wooden tables and chairs, set out in front, in a warm yellow glow. The only customer was a small, ancient, white-haired fellow who sat at one of the tables staring in a dismal fashion at a large tankard of ale set before him. He eyed Dick Palmer, as the latter rode up, with frank curiosity and, when the highwayman had handed over his steed to the ostler, called out: 'That's a fine courser you have there, young fella.'

Knowing this to be an invitation to join the old man at his table, Dick nodded and sat down opposite him.

'You're a stranger in these parts.'

Palmer nodded again.

'I am the Squire's groomsman,' said the old man in a grand, but rather unsteady voice.

An old, shabby woman appeared at the door of the inn. 'A quart of ale,' ordered Dick Palmer.

'You won't know, I suppose, the Squire — Squire Penfield?' grunted the old man.

'I have heard of him,' replied Palmer.

His companion took a copious draught from his tankard, then glanced quickly across at Palmer. 'You don't know my name,' he said in a somewhat secretive fashion. 'It's Benjamin Tapner.'

'Good evening,' said the highwayman. 'My name is Dick Palmer.'

'Good evenin',' replied Tapner thickly. He eyed Palmer a little suspiciously and then said slowly: 'I like the look of you, me lad.'

The woman appeared and placed the highwayman's ale on the table. Palmer gave her a coin and she muttered thanks and withdrew. Dick raised his tankard and cried: 'Your health, sir.'

'Yours,' said Tapner, and they drank deeply.

The old man banged his tankard down again, spilling some in the process, and then wiped his mouth and smacked his lips appreciatively. Suddenly he leant across the table, beckoning Dick Palmer to draw nearer.

'Listen, me lad, an' I'll tell you somethin',' said Tapner, rolling his eyes in a rather lugubrious fashion. 'Don't think,' he added in a louder tone, 'that what I tell you now be the ravings of a drunken old man. They ain't!'

Palmer shook his head solemnly and leaned closer.

'The Squire is married, you know.'

'So I believe,' commented Dick.

'Ah, but this you don't know — she's his second!'

Dick Palmer did not reply, but stared keenly at the wizened old groomsman and waited for him to continue.

'His first — she was French!'

Dick's eyes gleamed and he waited patiently whilst Tapner took another drink.

'Ha — now you are interested,' hissed the old man, noting Palmer's tense attitude. 'She was a fine lady,' he went on in a whisper, close to Dick's ear. 'Beautiful she was — dark and beautiful.'

Benjamin Tapner gazed rapturously into space. 'But he kept her locked in the Manor,' he breathed, his pale, watery eyes wide open, staring bleakly at Palmer. 'Wouldn't let her out!'

Tapner leaned back dramatically in his seat and watched to see what effect his words had had upon the highwayman. Dick Palmer was suitably impressed and curious to hear more. The old man leaned forward again, pushing his face beneath Palmer's and staring up at him in a cunning fashion. The highwayman could smell foul breath, but he dare not move away for fear of offending the old fellow.

'You wonder why — don't you?'

'Yes,' said Dick.

'Well, I don't know, but I do know this,' and Benjamin Tapner stuck out one long wrinkled finger and waved it about in front of Palmer's face. What the old man said next was in such a slurred whisper that the highwayman had to lean even closer to catch the words.

'I see'd her — not — for many — weeks,' mumbled Tapner. 'Then the Squire announces very coolly — she is dead — she has died of the small-pox!'

Benjamin Tapner slowly drew back and reached unsteadily for his tankard. But he never touched it. Instead he leaned forward again across the table.

'She have the small-pox!' he cried. 'It's foolish — she'd be the last to get it.' The old man reached for his tankard again, quaffed the ale, and rose slowly and laboriously from the table and, without another look at the highwayman, stumbled off towards the road, shaking his head sorrowfully. Dick Palmer remained at the table after he had gone, staring fixedly at the vacant chair. This was news indeed.

At last he strode off around the side of the inn in search of the stables. The ostler quickly fetched Red Ruby and in a minute Palmer was mounted and riding across the sward. He turned down the road towards Wake Manor. He guided the highly strung mare along the side of the road, on the grass, close in by the trees, so that they made no sound and seemed but a shadow in the darkness. There was no sign of Benjamin Tapner.

Dick wondered if the old man had fallen by the wayside and was now deep in drunken slumber. He soon forgot Tapner, however, at sight of the gates of the drive leading to Wake Manor. He crossed the road swiftly and entered the forest and threaded his way through the thick undergrowth towards the house. This time he approached from the north and thus, upon reaching the edge of the grounds, found himself some little way from the Manor. A light still shone from the window Will and he had watched earlier that day.

Palmer dismounted, patted Red Ruby's neck, and moved away around the edge of the forest towards the south where the trees grew close to the wall of the house. He darted across the drive and in a few moments was able to see straight into the lighted room. Palmer's black cloak blended well with the deep shadows beneath the trees and he was hardly visible.

But somebody, nevertheless, had seen the highwayman. He was leaning forward trying to make out who the occupants of the room were when a noise behind him disturbed him. Palmer swung round — but too late. A great figure leaped upon him and, before he was able to defend himself, two huge hands gripped his throat and began choking the very life from his body. Abruptly a second figure appeared and gave a hand to the first. Dick Palmer struggled wildly, but relentlessly he was borne to the ground. He fought like a tiger, trying to dislodge the terrible grip upon his throat, but it was of no use, and he found himself growing weaker.

Realising the futility of fighting against such odds and having no wish to die, Palmer stopped struggling and relaxed. The two men promptly sat on top of him. In the dim light the highwayman could faintly discern their features and one, a large ruffian, seemed familiar. The other rose and drew a pistol.

'Get up,' he snarled.

The big man jumped up and stepped aside and rather unsteadily Palmer got to his feet. They at once grasped each arm and shepherded him out onto the drive.

There the two men stared closely at Palmer.

'Ha!' cried the burly one.

'What is it?' asked the other.

'Nothing, nothing,' the first man muttered quickly. 'Let us take him to the Squire.'

Without more ado and a pistol in his back Palmer was led across the lawn and around the back of the Manor. On the way the highwayman brushed himself down, for he had become somewhat dishevelled, and he wished to look smart if he was to be presented to the Squire. He marched along quite cheerfully between his captors and the latter, noticing this, could but scowl with chagrin. Suddenly Palmer stopped as if struck by some thought.

'What's the matter?' growled the man with the pistol, prodding the weapon deep into the highwayman's back. Ignoring the fellow, Palmer cupped his hands about his mouth and, before the two men could do anything to stop him, gave out a strange, high-pitched call.

'What mischief is this?' cried the burly man.

Abruptly the sound of horse's hoofs, beating out a regular tattoo upon the ground, was heard. Palmer's captors swung about. A riderless horse galloped down the drive and disappeared out the gate. The two men listened in amazement to the sound of the hoofs as they faded into the night down old Epping Road.

'That was your steed,' said the burly man accusingly.

'That is true,' replied Dick Palmer cheerfully. 'You surely do not think I would leave her out here to catch cold?'

'Where has she gone?'

'Home!'

The two men gazed at him blankly at a loss to know what to do. At last, with muttered imprecations, they pushed Palmer forward again. Passing through a small door at rear of the house, they traversed innumerable dark passages before crossing a dimly-lit hall and arriving at a door beneath which a light shone.

Palmer guessed that this was the room into which he been trying to see before he was so rudely interrupted. The highwayman felt his heart beating, for now it seemed he was at last to meet Adam Penfield, the Squire of Wake Manor. The man with the pistol opened the door and pushed him in, keeping the pistol pressed deep into his back.

Standing by the window with his back to them was the Squire himself, and seated in a large armchair gazing studiously into a mirror held in her bejewelled hand, was his wife, Charlotte Penfield. At the back of the room, leaning against a large bookcase, was the man who — Palmer recognised him immediately — had shot at him outside the Black Horse Inn — Jack Gregory, the Squire's head warden.

'We found this man snooping in the bushes, sir.'

The Squire swung round, his pale, smooth features without expression. The light from the candles in the small chandelier above him shone in his dark eyes and on his black wig. Dick Palmer, however, was staring at Jack Gregory. The latter had started forward and was now gazing upon the highwayman in surprise.

Dick smiled and with an elaborate bow,

said: 'Good evening to you, Gregory, my friend.'

The Squire frowned slightly at this for he knew not what went on, and then Gregory, his little eyes gleaming triumphantly, crossed the room to his master and whispered in his ear. Adam Penfield raised his thin eyebrows in mild surprise on hearing what Gregory had to say and gazed searchingly at Palmer. The Squire suddenly beckoned to the burly fellow standing guard at Palmer's side. The man ran clumsily across the room and stood before the Squire, fearful and obedient. Penfield indicated Palmer with one slim finger and then addressed a question to the man in a low voice. The big fellow nodded his head energetically in reply. The Squire waved him away and then strode across the room to Dick Palmer.

'So — you are the villain who killed my poor servant, Simon Beckley?'

Palmer smiled lazily, for he was not fooled by the Squire's tone. Instead of replying to the question, he said: 'Tell me, Squire — do you usually let these two men of yours' — Palmer pointed at Jack

115

Gregory and the man the Squire had just spoken to — 'do you usually let them run around attacking innocent innkeepers and their daughters?'

Silence fell upon the room. Dick Palmer thoroughly enjoyed it. Jack Gregory's little eyes were darting about the room in consternation, but the Squire stood motionless staring fixedly at Palmer. The highwayman was not put out, however, though he could still feel the uncomfortable pressure of the pistol in his back held by the small man. At last Penfield spoke — in a cold, unemotional tone: 'What is your name, boy?' he asked.

Dick Palmer thought quickly — he preferred to keep his name secret for the time being. Then he had an idea. 'My name, sir? Why, it's 'The Son of Dick Turpin'!'

'The Son of Dick Turpin?' cried the burly man, gazing wide-eyed at Palmer.

Adam Penfield drummed his manicured nails on a small table in annoyance. Dick Palmer's words had created quite a stir in the room for the name of Turpin was synonymous with infamous devilry

116

and was known throughout the land.

'Hold your tongue, Bullard,' the Squire cried. 'Have you never heard of the name before?' Penfield turned angrily towards Gregory. 'Saddle the horses. We leave for Loughton this night to hand over this rogue to the Constable!' The warden promptly left the room on his mission. The Squire then turned back to Bullard. 'Tie his hands behind his back, fool,' he commanded, 'and collect his weapons.'

This was soon done and a few moments later Dick Palmer was marched outside to the front of the Manor, the Squire close behind. Almost at the same time the short figure of Jack Gregory appeared out of the dark leading three horses. Adam Penfield mounted immediately and then Bullard and Gregory helped Palmer into the saddle.

Gregory mounted and took the reins of Palmer's steed and they set off down the drive. Dick Palmer still did not feel perturbed, but he knew there was little chance of escape at the present moment. In any case he wished to find out more about the affairs of the Squire before he contemplated this move.

'Tell me, young man,' said the Squire affably, as they trotted down the road towards High Beach. 'Why did you kill my servant?'

Palmer smiled and glanced at Penfield, trying to read the man's thoughts, but his pale countenance was blank.

'I did not,' the highwayman replied blandly, adding: 'but I seek the man who did.'

The Squire smiled. 'I fear the jury will not believe that.'

Palmer did not bother to make any answer to this remark and they rode on in silence. Jack Gregory, staring straight ahead down the dark road, held the reins of Palmer's horse in a firm grip and the highwayman realised the head warden was on the alert for any bid he might make for freedom.

Dick turned to Penfield again. 'Tell me this, Squire,' he said in a quiet tone. 'Of what did your first wife die?'

The start Adam Penfield gave was unmistakable and for a second he lost control of his steed and the animal began prancing about the road in a wild manner. The Squire cursed and pulled hard on the reins and at last he regained control. He turned to Palmer and the highwayman drew in his breath quickly, for Adam Penfield had also lost his composure. His face had turned livid, his skin had become creased and lined in a hideous manner, and his dark eyes glittered like a snake's. The change was so abrupt that Palmer could but stare at him in amazement.

'You meddlesome fool,' the Squire screamed. Quickly he raised his heavy whip and lashed it viciously across the highwayman's face. Palmer fell back and nearly tumbled from his horse, and a terrible stinging pain shot across his forehead, so that he was much put out to restrain the cry of agony that sprang to his lips. He bowed his head forward trying to hide from the two men his expression of pain.

'I will have you strung from the gibbet,' the Squire cried shrilly, 'until that prying nose of yours falls from your snivelling face!'

Palmer could see that Penfield was in two minds whether to repeat his action, but he did not, and the highwayman sighed with relief for he knew he could not stand that kind of treatment very long. A little while later they entered High Beach. They passed through without incident and were soon deep in the forest again. Gradually the pain across Palmer's forehead subsided and now his eyes gleamed triumphantly — there was, then, something strange about the death of the Squire's first wife. Penfield's countenance was filled with a virulent scowl, but he was not disposed to talk and appeared now to be in a greater hurry than before to reach Loughton and hand Palmer over to the Chief Constable.

They broke into a canter and the old clock in the church tower was striking eleven when they entered the town of Loughton. They stopped before a house on the edge of the town and the Squire dismounted and went and rapped on the door. After some while a man appeared, scowling, and Dick recognized Pucky, the Chief Constable. Adam Penfield spoke to him in a confidential tone for some minutes.

The Constable looked up, when the Squire had finished, gazed through the darkness at the two horsemen and delight filled his big, red face. 'Excellent, Penfield,' he cried. 'One moment and I will be with you.'

Pucky disappeared into the house and Palmer heard the rattling of keys. He then reappeared carrying a lamp and a big bunch of keys. He led the way round to the back of the house. Gregory dismounted and grasped the reins of the three horses and followed Pucky and the Squire. A small, black stone building stood at the rear of the house on the edge of a field.

Pucky unlocked the heavy iron door of the building. The Squire then crossed over to Dick Palmer, still seated in the saddle. He gave the highwayman a rough push and Palmer tumbled to the ground, his head crashing violently on the ground.

'Get up,' Penfield snarled.

Palmer gained his feet a little unsteadily for he was half stunned. The Squire and

Gregory grasped him and pushed him into the prison. Inside were four cells facing one another. The Constable unlocked the iron-barred gate of one, and the Squire, with a heavy kick, sent the highwayman reeling inside. The gate closed with a clang.

'I will deal with you, my fine rascal, on the morrow,' the Constable cried. Then the three men strode outside again, the iron door closed and Palmer heard the key turn in the massive lock.

8

Dick Palmer spent a sleepless night on the bare stone floor of the cell and in the morning he arose with stiff limbs and an aching side. His head throbbed painfully and tenderly he felt the red weal that stretched across his forehead as a result of the blow the Squire had dealt him with his whip.

The cell was small and the stone walls damp and rough. High up on one side, just below the black ceiling, was a small barred window through which a ray of light came from the rising sun. This window, Palmer surmised, looked out over the field at the back of the little prison. There was no furniture and Palmer began wondering how long he would have to stay in the place.

His optimistic cheerfulness of the night before had gone and he was very depressed, for the future looked black. He sat down on the floor again and stared grimly up at the tiny window. It was out of his reach — in any case the two iron bars looked strong enough. If they had not been there he might have just squeezed through, but they were there and that was the end of it.

Dick Palmer pursed his lips and looked dejectedly around the walls, but there was no escape there either for they must have been a foot in thickness. Suddenly he heard the prison door open and footsteps come down the passage. The Chief Constable came into view. He gazed in through the iron bars, his red face grimly set.

'So it was you who killed Simon Beckley,' he grunted.

Dick Palmer glared at him and scrambled to his feet. 'No it was not,' he cried hotly. 'He was shot before my very eyes and the pistol was thrown into the room.'

'Ha — the Squire said you might tell some such tale!'

Dick's eyes gleamed. 'Did he? And how does he know — I didn't tell him?' replied Dick.

The Constable shrugged his tall frame and then scratched his fair wig. 'It is not important. You are guilty. There is no doubt. Prepare yourself. At noon we set out for London — and Tyburn gallows!'

Palmer did not answer.

Pucky stared at the highwayman for several seconds and then he turned and marched down the passage and out of the prison, closing the iron door with a heavy clang behind him.

The Constable's first remark gave Palmer some food for thought and for a short while he almost forgot he was imprisoned and soon to finish his career on the end of a rope. Adam Penfield was connected with the murder, then, after all — how else could he know exactly what happened? Jeanette Murray was the only person, other than himself, who knew a pistol had been thrown into the room, and Dick knew she would not tell the Squire. The highwayman felt somewhat pleased with himself. His suspicions that the murder and the attacks on Jeanette were connected, seemed to be correct. The Squire of Wake Manor knew something about both affairs.

Then there was the strange death of Penfield's first wife — strange according to Benjamin Tapner. Yes, here was a pretty mystery. The highwayman was deep in thought when there came a sudden interruption.

'Dick!'

The whisper came from high up in the wall. The highwayman started and then leaped excitedly to his feet and gazed up at the barred window. Framed there was the large, tanned face of Will Snell, an expansive grin upon his lips.

'Will!'

'What are you doing down there, friend?'

Dick's heart thrilled with joy and he laughed happily. 'I don't know, Will.'

Wild Will shook his head in a despairing fashion. 'As soon as I saw Red Ruby come trotting in,' he grunted, 'I knew something had gone wrong.' He stared down thoughtfully at Palmer and then at the iron bars before him, and in a sudden fit of anger, grasped them and pulled with all his might. But they remained firm.

A hopeless expression filled Dick's face. 'Can't you break them, Will?' The giant shook his head grimly. Palmer gazed desperately around the tiny cell, but it was no good — the window was the only likely avenue of escape.

'There must be some way,' murmured Will Snell. He grasped one of the bars with both hands and Dick Palmer saw him grit his teeth, tense his great muscles and pull with all his strength. The prisoner watched anxiously and with beating heart as he saw the veins on Will's forehead stand out like rope and his face slowly turn deep crimson. But the bar failed to move.

'Have you brought the horses?' asked Dick suddenly.

Will relaxed and stepped back, breathing heavily. 'Yes, but I fear to bring them close. It's completely open here. I have left them by the pond yonder.'

Dick sighed dismally and then Will began pulling at the iron bar again. Something dropped upon the prisoner's head and fell to the floor with a soft clink. He picked it up and stared at it — it was a small piece of broken mortar.

'Will,' cried Dick, 'keep on — keep on, some mortar has fallen.'

The giant's eyes gleamed and he renewed his efforts. Palmer, standing below, watched in fascination as he saw the great knuckles grow white and the huge rugged face strain and redden as Will, breathing heavily like an overladen cart horse, exerted all his mighty strength on the iron bar.

More pieces of mortar broke off and fell to the floor and Dick Palmer's excitement mounted. At last Will had to stop to gain his breath and for a moment his face disappeared from the opening. Five minutes passed by during which Dick listened with trepidation for sounds of the Chief Constable returning to the prison. But all was quiet, and if Pucky kept his word and did not return until noon, then they were safe for more than an hour.

The massive hands and wrists appeared again and grasped the bar, but Will's face still remained out of sight. The highway-man knew that this was to be the last effort. If it failed — then they would have to think of something else, but time would then be against them. Obtaining a firm grip Will's bearded face appeared again, this time grimly set.

Palmer realised now what his friend intended to try and do — pull out the bar with one tremendous heave. Dick waited breathlessly. The knuckles suddenly whitened, the wrist stretched and the fingers flattened against the bar. Wild Will screwed up his face — and pulled. There was a loud, crumbling noise and the giant's face disappeared from the cell window — and with him went the iron bar!

Dick Palmer jumped up and down excitedly, clapping his hands like a schoolboy, heedless of the noise he made. Will Snell's face appeared again, grinning broadly. Suddenly Palmer sobered, for there was still the second bar to be removed. He could not escape yet — the space was far too narrow.

Wild Will glared ferociously at the second iron bar and grasped it aggressively.

Then a surprising thing happened. Before the giant could exert his full strength, the bar came away in his hands! Will stared at it unbelievingly and Dick's eyes nearly popped from his head. Abruptly they both burst out laughing. It was obvious what had happened — the removal of the first bar had loosened the second.

'Quick!' cried Will.

He pushed his arms through the tiny window and Palmer ran forward and grasped them. Will then drew back and pulled Dick up the side of the cell wall. In a minute the young highwayman had squeezed through and the two of them were crouching down by the prison wall on the edge of the field, out of sight of the Constable's house.

Without a word Will lay down flat upon the soft ploughed earth and, waving to Palmer to do the same, began crawling out across the field. Dick dropped to the ground quickly and followed close behind. It was hard work; and they had to rest in a deep furrow when half way to the forest. Palmer glanced back and could just see the top of Pucky's house — the field, after a level stretch, made a slight descent to the edge of the forest. In a minute or so they should be able to regain their feet and make a run for the cover of the trees.

Will had no intention, however, of spoiling things now they had got so far by any premature move, and he carried on until they were well out of sight of the prison. Then, glancing behind at Palmer to warn him to prepare himself, he suddenly leaped to his feet and ran like a rampaging bull for the cover of the trees. Palmer was quick to follow, and a second later they were panting heavily and grinning delightedly at one another in the sanctuary of Epping Forest.

They gazed back across the field towards the prison, but all seemed quiet — Palmer's escape had not as yet been discovered. The two men were glad to see each other again and Dick shook Will's hand enthusiastically.

'Come, let us get right away,' Will grunted. 'The more space we put between us and that prison the better.'

He turned and led the way through the forest to the little pond near the Loughton Road, where their horses were tethered. Red Ruby gave a whinny of pleasure at sight of her master and the highwayman patted his steed affection-ately. They mounted immediately and, keeping a lookout for any signs of pursuit, rode back through the forest towards the cave. On the way Palmer told of his adventures since his parting from Will following their visit together to Wake Manor.

'What's the reason for these things?' asked the giant.

'The Squire has some scheme afoot, that is certain. But what, I am as yet not sure.' The last few words Palmer said quite thoughtfully, almost to himself, and Will guessed that Dick had his own ideas on the subject, but was not ready at the present moment to divulge them.

They had circled High Beach, and were now riding along the edge of the Loughton Road. Both men were deep in thought as they cantered along and, as a consequence, failed to see the horseman in the shadows under the trees on the far side of the road.

'Hold your steeds, good gentlemen,' came the cry. 'I would lighten you of your silver!'

Will and Dick glanced up quickly and jerked their horses to a standstill. They stared in amazement at the newcomer who had now ridden forward into the centre of the road. He was a long, thin fellow with mousy hair and dirty clothes, and across his forehead there stretched a narrow grey scar.

There was a dead silence. Then suddenly Will Snell, throwing back his head, burst into a loud roar of laughter. At this the man frowned and looked puzzled, for this was indeed strange behaviour upon being held up on the high road.

'Nay, nay, lanky,' cried Will, cackling like a hen, 'brother cannot rob brother — lower your pistol!'

The highwayman stared at him in an even more puzzled fashion. 'What do you mean?' he asked.

'I mean,' said Will, 'that I and my

excellent friend here ply the same delicate profession as your good self.'

'Aha,' said the man, light dawning in his pale eyes. 'I now understand you.' Slowly a smile broke out on his lips.

'Come — put away your weapon,' Will said. He leaned across to Dick and whispered something in his ear. The young highwayman nodded. 'Listen, friend,' Will added, 'why not join us — we know of a pleasant nook and go there now to fill our bellies?'

Dick nodded cordially. 'It's as my friend says,' he exclaimed. 'Come — join us.'

The newcomer looked a little suspicious, then he shrugged his shoulders and returned his pistol to his pocket. 'A kind invitation — that I must admit,' he said a little doubtfully. At last he smiled. 'I cannot say from whence my next meal might come — I accept your offer gladly.'

'Good,' replied Will. 'My name is Will Snell and this is Dick Palmer — and yours, sir?'

'Rob Welton,' the stranger told them.

'Then follow us,' cried Wild Will, 'and

this day we will eat and drink as befits the King himself.'

Without more ado Will and Dick dug in their spurs and galloped off down the road and Welton, after a curious look at the pair, followed a little way behind. Will Snell kept up a loud and cheerful conversation as they rode along, and they approached the cave in great spirits, even Welton was smiling for none could resist the humorous tales Will told.

'I remember an old fellow who dreaded the day he might meet a gentleman of the road,' Will remarked as they came out at the top of the valley. 'Such was his fear that he always carried with him on his travels two purses — one full with his money and valuables and the other almost empty.

'Well, as you might guess, at last he did come face to face with a highwayman on a deserted heath — and, believe it or not, it was Captain James Hind himself!

'The old fellow promptly handed over his purse and then rode off well pleased with himself. But — terrible calamity! He suddenly discovered that instead of giving

Captain Hind his half-empty purse as he had thought he had done — he had given the highwayman the full one!

'Back he rode after Hind at great speed and, catching him, he declared the purse he had given the Captain was of great sentimental value — would he accept this one in exchange? 'Willingly', says Hind, being the gentleman he was and the exchange was duly carried out. Off went the old fellow, highly elated. When out of sight he greedily felt for his purse and opened it. The poor old fellow nearly fell off his horse with the shock. It was empty! The good Captain, being the kind of man that he was, had already taken the silver!'

Will Snell tethered his horse to the pole wedged between the outjuttings of rock outside the cave and then went inside, telling his friends to be seated in the glade. Dick followed him in, however, and filled three tankards with ale and took them outside.

It was not long after that a roasted pig revolved upon the spit and the three men were feeding right royally. As mid-afternoon approached the sun warmed to its job and beat down relentlessly upon the forest, and the three highwaymen rested after their repast and lay at ease in the shadow of the bushes.

Rob Welton told little about himself and Dick and Will were not disposed to ask him for they were not curious, and thus the three of them came to a mutual understanding not to mention each other's private affairs.

Welton uncurled his long, wiry frame and stood up. 'I think I will bathe in the stream yonder,' he said, 'for I feel very dirty.'

'Fine idea,' grunted Dick, yawning.

When he had gone Will turned to Palmer and said: 'So the Squire, it appears, is behind everything?'

'So it seems.'

'I remember you mentioned that Simon Beckley tried to speak of him before he died.'

'Yes, but he died before he could tell what he knew. Well might it have been about the Squire's first wife.'

'Ha — you have something there.'

'A likelihood I fancy. But why these

attacks upon Jeantette — that is, Miss Murray?'

'The rascal obviously seeks something of value — murder and robbery are a means to an end.'

'Yes, I agree with you,' Dick remarked and then added: 'I hope to gain further information when I have had a look at something tomorrow.'

Rob Welton pushed through the thicket at this moment, looking greatly refreshed, his grey, wiry hair glinting in the sun. 'Now I feel better,' cried he.

He lay down upon the grass with a contented sigh and composed himself for sleep and not long afterwards they were all happily snoring. Suddenly Wild Will sat up and broke the peaceful silence with his powerful voice.

'How do you gentlemen fancy wild duck roasted for your meal tonight?'

Palmer opened his eyes at once. 'A fine idea,' he cried.

'Then, my friends, let's sleep well, for when the sun sets we must repair to the lowlands. This eve we shall sup like lords!'

The forest life was in full swing as the

three highwaymen closed their eyes again. In a few moments they were dreaming of a delicious aroma and of a fat golden duck roasting on the spit above a crackling fire.

And so it was.

9

Dick Palmer next morning awoke with a start. He frowned up at the black ceiling of the cave, trying to recollect what had disturbed him. Ah — now he remembered. He had been dreaming about Jeanette Murray! He grinned to himself and sat up. The sun streamed in through the mouth of the cave and Palmer suddenly realised that they had all slept late — due, no doubt, to the huge feast they had eaten the night before.

Will Snell lay stretched out upon the hay, snoring loudly, his mouth wide open. As he exhaled his wiry, red beard quivered like the bushes on the slopes of some angry volcano. Rob Welton was sleeping peacefully upon the far side of the cave. Dick Palmer leaned towards Wild Will and grasped the big fellow's nose between his forefinger and thumb, and squeezed!

Will sat up and gave a loud howl and

his arms flailed the air like the arms of a windmill. One swinging fist caught Dick unawares on the side of his head and sent him sprawling forward to the mouth of the cave. The young highwayman came to rest with his head between his legs.

'Avast!' roared Will Snell, still half asleep, 'you yellow scum — advance and I will flatten the lot of you!' He blinked in an owlish fashion around the cave and then saw Dick Palmer.

'Nay, Dick,' he cried, 'but you look exceedingly uncomfortable — do you usually sleep in such a strange position?'

Palmer uncurled himself and glared ferociously at his friend. 'Dullard!' he roared, 'You dealt me a blow!'

'I?' queried Will in surprise.

'You,' growled Palmer.

'How was that?'

'You were in the throes of some nightmare.'

'Oh — ah yes, I remember. A lovely dream,' replied Will. 'I was just about to do battle with the entire French army!'

Palmer grunted in disgust. 'Come, it's late,' he said. 'Let's prepare the meal. I'm hungry and soon must leave.'

'Ha, ha,' cried Will, rubbing his eyes and giving his young friend a knowing look.

Will Snell stood up, gave a great yawn and then helped Dick Palmer to prepare breakfast. The orange sun was spreading out over the tops of the trees when at last the smell of fried bacon wafted on the breeze and reached the nostrils of Rob Welton still asleep in the cave. He awoke and sat up and sniffed the air like a thoroughbred, and in a minute came running out licking his lips in a ravenous fashion

'You appear hungry, Rob,' greeted Palmer.

'You speak words of great truth,' grunted the highwayman, sitting down upon the ground and starting eating. In a little while the sound of the crunching of jaws mingled with the singing of the birds in the nearby thicket and with the rippling of the stream as it flowed down through the valley.

Dick Palmer hurried over his meal and finished well before the others. He rose and patted his stomach in a contented manner. 'That part of me at least is satisfied,' he cried, and turned and stepped lightheartedly across to Red Ruby. He saddled the mare, mounted and was ready for the road. He waved cheerfully to his two friends, still eating, and then spurred forward through the bushes. Will waved back without looking up and soon Palmer was out of sight at the top of the valley. Here he dismounted and, kneeling by the edge of the stream, bathed his face in the clear, sparkling waters.

He jumped to his feet again, refreshed, and regaining the saddle, continued on his way. As he rode Dick kept a sharp lookout for any of the Constable's or Squire's men. In future he intended to take more care. 'If I'm taken,' he murmured in Red Ruby's ear, 'it will be for the burial service. I'll give a look to me pistol — ah, the flint is all safe. Now I'm ready for the Squire himself.'

He crossed the Loughton Road some distance from the village and rode around through the forest towards the Black

Horse Inn. As he approached the back of the stables the sound of splashing water reached his ears. He dismounted and crept steadily forward, pistol at the ready, and reached the back of one of the stables. He peered cautiously around the corner into the yard and there beheld a very pleasant scene.

Jeanette Murray, a pretty apron round her slim waist and a red cap perched on the top of her black hair, was bent over a large tub outside the kitchen door, washing her delicate garments. Dick Palmer watched for some time, taking in every little detail of the girl's profile, until at last he wearied of just watching her and wished to be near her. Suddenly he put his fingers to his lips and gave a low whistle. Jeanette looked up like a startled fawn and gazed quickly about the yard, a frown creasing her lovely forehead.

All at once she saw Dick Palmer's face peering round the corner of the stable and she gave an audible gasp, her hand flew to her lips and she looked down at herself in consternation. She glanced up at Dick again and then abruptly turned and dashed inside the house.

At first Palmer felt a little disappointed and then he realised what women were like and he grinned in a knowledgeable way and settled down to await her reappearance. Time passed by and still she did not come and Palmer began to get a little worried. Surely she did not need all this time to get ready? Perhaps Adam Penfield was in the Black Horse and was even now preparing to attack him.

But, as he felt deep down, there was no need for his anxiety. The door opened at last and she appeared on the threshold and stood there hesitantly. Dick Palmer took a long deep breath and gazed upon her with awe and admiration, She looked very beautiful now — the highwayman could but marvel at her loveliness. She had changed into a black gown, which clung tightly to her body and fell in soft folds from her hips.

She hurried across the yard towards him and Palmer retreated a little into the forest. When she reached him she was a little out of breath.

'You have escaped,' she gasped.

'Ah — you heard, then. Yes, with the help of Will Snell. Let us go deeper into the forest. It is safer.' Palmer took her arm and led the way towards the glade they had visited before. They sat down upon the bank and gazed upon one another.

'How is your father?' Dick asked.

'He is lots better, thank you.'

'Good.'

'You know it's very dangerous. The Constable has a dozen men out looking for you and the Squire is helping him as much as he can. They came to the inn very early this morning to warn us to look out for you.'

'So the Squire hunts me as well. I expected that.'

'Your forehead,' cried she, suddenly noticing the weal, caused by the Squire's whip. 'Oh dear, what has occurred?'

Palmer told her briefly of what had taken place on the way to Loughton prison. She leaned forward and clasped his head gently in her hands and a lingering perfume stole into Palmer's nostrils, so that he felt a little dizzy.

'You must take care,' she breathed and

she kissed his forehead. 'Tell me, have you stopped playing the game of High Toby?'

'We — ll,' replied Dick, somewhat hesitantly, 'we — we haven't quite yet!'

'Why not?' cried she. 'You must — it will not assist you and will bring only evil results.'

Jeanette was annoyed and her dark eyes flashed like a ray of sunlight catching the crest of an ocean wave. She tossed her head angrily and a lock of hair fell down and hid one cheek.

'I am hunted — what else can I do?' he asked.

'There is no call to rob innocent people.'

'I have only robbed once — and that was the Chief Constable.'

Jeanette stared at him as if he were mad. 'The Chief Constable?' she cried. 'You are a fool. I refuse to consort with a man who carries on such a wicked practice. It's the lowest of the low!'

It dawned upon the highwayman that she was really annoyed. He drew nearer her, but she moved away along the bank, her nose in the air, refusing to look at him.

'We must eat,' Dick pleaded.

But she continued to ignore him and began to play with the edge of her dress, smoothing out the material with one slim hand.

'There are three of us now,' Dick informed her. 'A fellow named Rob Welton has joined us. How can we survive without money with which to procure food?'

She turned abruptly upon him. 'It's of no avail to make excuses — Who is this Rob Welton?'

'He tried to rob Will and me upon our departure from prison. It was funny. We invited him back to the cave. He's a quiet fellow and long in the limb.'

'He might be a spy of the Squire's.'

'I doubt it.'

'Three highwaymen skulking in a cave,' said she contemptuously. 'Would *you* be pleased if you were robbed?'

'I don't know — I haven't had that pleasure yet!'

She gave him a dark look, which Dick thought was very pretty, and then rose to her feet and gazed disdainfully down upon him.

'I must return — I have a lot of work to do,' she said and she turned and stepped lightly through the trees towards the inn. Dick scrambled to his feet and ran hastily after her.

'So soon?' cried he.

'Yes,' she replied without turning.

'I shall come again,' Dick called, as she entered the yard. But she gave no reply.

With a somewhat melancholy feeling Dick Palmer returned to Red Ruby and mounted and rode slowly back towards the hideout. He suddenly realised he had not told her about his meeting with Benjamin Tapner and of what the old man had said, but it could wait until next time. Dick felt quite annoyed with the girl for some reason and his thoughts were upon her continuously on the journey back to the cave.

The sun was already high in the sky and blazing down upon the forest and Palmer realised that afternoon would be very hot. By the time he had reached the cave, his shirt was exceedingly damp and stuck to his body in a most uncomfortable manner. Will was astride a rock by the fire, stripped to the waist, preparing a joint of meat. His great muscles, drenched with sweat, glistened in the sun.

'Aha — now that is a fine idea!' cried Palmer and he promptly divested himself of his upper garments. He tethered Red Ruby to the pole wedged between the two outjuttings of rock and brought her water from the stream. The mare gave a shrill whinny of pleasure and then plunged her nose deep into the cool liquid.

Rob Welton lay asleep at the mouth of the cave, his long frame stretching half way across the den. Palmer joined Will Snell at the fireside and assisted him with the preparations for the midday meal.

'Seems to me, Will,' quoth Dick, 'that you are for ever preparing food for us hungry beasts.'

'Hungry beasts you are and there is no doubt,' grunted Will. 'But I must admit I like this kind of job.'

'It's lucky for Rob and me that you do!'

The sun rose higher and reached its zenith and at last Will, sweating like a horse, had finished and dinner was ready. Thereupon they set to and filled their stomachs and silence reigned. They crawled away into the shade when they had finished and went to sleep. It was too hot to do anything else.

Wild Will was having a very pleasant dream when Dick Palmer suddenly awakened and sat up. 'I have an idea,' cried he.

'You may keep it,' grunted Will, 'It's too hot for such things.'

'You know yonder pond between the village and Loughton, near the highway?'

'I do,' said Will, beginning to snore again.

'I think I will go for a swim!'

Slowly, with great effort, Will Snell raised himself upon one arm and gazed with pained incredulity at his young friend. 'Has the sun affected you?' he asked. 'It's a foolish practice.'

'I'm going,' replied Palmer and no sooner said than done, he had jumped to his feet and began saddling Red Ruby. Within a minute he was ready and leaping into the saddle, he rode swiftly out of the den. Will Snell shook his head sadly. Then he called out: 'Remember, you ride in hostile country.'

'I remember,' Palmer called back over

the bushes. 'Don't worry they will not take me again.' And then he was gone, cantering up the slope of the valley. Wild Will shrugged his shoulders, lay back again and soon was snoring lustily.

In the forest, beneath the canopy of leaves, the heat was stifling and Palmer was glad he had discarded his top clothes. Once, when he approached too near the road, he espied two villagers walking leisurely towards High Beach, and he immediately rode deeper into the forest. Thus it was some time before he reached the pond. In fact he was beginning to wonder whether he had lost his way when he suddenly broke through a tall thicket and saw the water ahead, glittering between the trees like a precious jewel. He galloped forward to the edge and dismounted. Quickly he tied Red Ruby to a tree and, after a careful look around, divested himself of his lower garments and stepped to the bank. Gingerly he slid into the water.

Ah! What luxury! What pure joy! How heavenly it was — the highwayman splashed and jumped about with infinite delight. The water slipped caressingly around his limbs, soothing him and engendering a tranquil, lazy feeling the like of which he had not experienced for many a day. The forest formed a dark green fringe around the pond, in complete contrast to the bright green of the banks and the glinting surface of the water, and Palmer felt as if he were lying in some sun-kissed haven set in the middle of a hostile, gloomy land.

But the dream-like harmonious state into which he had fallen was abruptly disturbed by a loud, gruff voice.

'It's very convenient of you, my friend — do you mind if I lighten your pockets whilst you bathe?'

Dick Palmer lowered his feet quickly to the bottom of the pond and stood up and stared with surprise and rising anger at the masked horseman who had suddenly appeared at the edge of the bank. The fellow wore a great, black, flowing cloak and a large, sweeping three-cornered hat — because of the latter and a small black mask Palmer could see little of his features.

The newcomer brandished a pistol

warningly as he rode across to the small pile of clothes. He dismounted and, still displaying the pistol and watching Palmer warily, picked up the highwayman's breeches and turned them upside down, emptying the contents upon the grass.

Dick's face turned purple with rage and he made as if to wade out of the pond. The robber jumped with fright and waved the pistol about in a threatening manner. Palmer gritted his teeth, but halted and the robber, with added haste, picked up all that he could.

Dick Palmer watched these proceedings with eyes that blazed with savage fury and such was his ferocious appearance that the robber glanced at him a little apprehensively. The intrusion had jolted Palmer out of his dream world in which he had been revelling and he did not like it. The robber hurriedly picked up the remaining articles and, with a rather perturbed glance at the solitary figure standing waist high in the water staring fixedly at him, ran to his steed, mounted and galloped off swiftly towards the Loughton Road.

Immediately he was gone, Dick Palmer waded quickly to the bank, scrambled up and raced across to his clothes. In a minute he was dressed and running towards Red Ruby. The mare saw him coming and, sensing her master's urgency, she tensed her powerful frame and as soon as Palmer was seated in the saddle, leaped forward like a great hound.

They thundered around the edge of the pond and careered through the narrow stretch of forest between the glade and the highway, the thud of Red Ruby's hoofs upon the ground sounding like the beat of a drum. Dick Palmer bent low over his steed and spurred her on, and the grim set of his mouth and the glint in his eyes boded ill for the robber.

10

Flashing across the Loughton Road
Palmer plunged into the forest upon the
far side, sweeping in and out between the
trees and bushes. He could hear, in the
distance, the crashing of twigs as the
robber galloped away, but the highwayman was not troubled for he knew the
robber's grey mare was no match for Red
Ruby.

Dick patted his steed's mane and
whispered words of encouragement in her
ear, and the magnificent horse flicked
back her ears and stretched out her neck
and went through the forest like a
thunderbolt. A stranger who might have
happened upon the pair at that moment
would but have marvelled at the rider's
great skill and the masterly way with
which he handled the mare along the
tortuous paths.

Dick Palmer gained rapidly upon the
masked robber and before many minutes

had passed the fellow was glancing behind in an anxious manner and frantically spurring his horse to even greater efforts. But the grey mare did not have it in her, she had reached her limit, and Palmer drew closer. The highwayman kept well down in the saddle for he expected the robber at any moment to draw his pistol, but the man appeared to realise the futility of firing at such a pace and instead he concentrated upon obtaining the last ounce of speed from his grey mare.

Dick was not fifty paces behind now and the robber glanced back every few seconds, and by his demeanour he was obviously greatly frightened. On and on they went thundering through the forest, darting like shadows across the pools of sunlight, plunging again into the weird half-light beneath the trees.

The robber cast one more anxious glance back over his shoulder and, as he did so, a low hanging branch swept across his path. He faced the front again and saw his danger, but he was too late to avoid it and he gave a shrill scream of terror as the branch caught him across the waist and sent him spinning from the saddle.

Dick Palmer pulled hard on the reins and they slithered to a halt, the chestnut mare shying in surprise at the abruptness of the action. The robber had fallen near the trunk of a tree and Palmer dismounted quickly and ran across to him.

'Rise, cowardly footpad,' he cried, drawing his pistol.

But the robber did not stir — the fall apparently had stunned him. Palmer replaced his pistol in his belt, stepped up to the fellow's side and reaching forward with both hands, tore away the mask and hat.

The young highwayman uttered a stifled gasp and fell to one knee, icy fingers clutching at his heart, for the lovely white face of Jeanette Murray stared up at him! 'Jeanette,' he breathed in horror. 'Jeanette!' A terrible feeling of remorse swept over him as he shook her frantically. Almost immediately, however, she stirred, her long eyelashes fluttered open and she gazed up at him wonderingly.

'Oh Dick,' she murmured, 'you did frighten me so.'

The highwayman heaved a great sigh of relief. 'Ah, Jeanette — Jeanette, how can I seek forgiveness? How could I know it was you?'

She smiled slightly. 'You were not supposed to,' she replied, a twinkle in her eyes. 'I thought I would teach you a lesson, but I'm afraid I, instead, have been taught one!'

Suddenly she sat up, disengaging herself from his arms. She rubbed her side ruefully. 'Ah, but it's very sore,' she murmured. Dick leaned forward and rubbed the spot for her. Jeanette felt in the pockets of her riding cloak and withdrew the various articles she had stolen from the highwayman.

'Here,' said she. 'The spoils of my robbery — I return them with compliments,' and she laughed gaily. Full of repentance Dick took them and replaced them in his pockets, feeling somewhat sheepish.

'Now you know what it is like to be robbed,' she said sternly, lying back in the grass and gazing up at him.

'I promise to cease,' Dick said in earnest, 'directly I have solved the mystery surrounding you and discovered, as well, who killed Simon Beckley.'

She looked at him thoughtfully. 'All right, but — ' and she wagged one slim finger at him ' — mind you do or there shall be trouble!'

'As you wish,' replied Palmer obediently, and he leaned over and kissed her. At that moment he remembered he had not told her of what Benjamin Tapner had said about the Squire's first wife, and thereupon he proceeded to relate the incident to her in some detail.

'Ah,' Jeanette commented at the end. 'The picture of our dear Squire grows blacker and more incomprehensible every day. I wonder what wicked scheme he has in hand?'

'Whatever it is, you are part of it. So be careful — never venture abroad unless you are well protected.'

'Yes, I will do as you say, but it is all very strange and mysterious.'

The highwayman picked up her cloak,

hat and mask, rolled them into a bundle and then went and tied them to her saddle. He came back and sat down, and they remained silent and listened to the singing of the birds high up in the leafy canopy above. The grass around them was a rich green and dappled by the odd ray of sunlight that came slanting down through the thick foliage.

'What is the prison like in Loughton?' asked she suddenly.

'Damp and cold,' Dick grunted.

Jeanette caressed the weal upon Palmer's forehead. 'Adam Penfield is a nasty fellow,' she said in a low voice, and then added: 'He is not liked by the villagers you know. He treats them as if they were fools and his servants as if they were his slaves.'

'Yes, that I have heard. But he is a cunning fellow and we must take every care to ensure that he doesn't get what he is after.'

'It was foolish of you to visit him by yourself,' said she. 'You have a tempestuous nature.'

Palmer glanced sideways at her, but

161

there was a twinkle in her eyes. He grinned. 'It can't be helped.'

They became quiet again, sitting happily side by side. The afternoon quickly passed away and at last Jeannette rose to her feet. 'I must be gone,' she exclaimed, 'my father will wonder what has become of me.'

'As you say,' Dick replied without enthusiasm.

They rose and together mounted their horses and made their way, by a circuitous route, through the forest towards the Black Horse Inn. Behind the stables they parted and Dick watched Jeanette ride into the yard and hand her horse to the ostler. Then the highwayman swung Red Ruby about and set off back to the cave.

When he arrived at the hideout, Dick found Will Snell cooking again and he immediately gave his big friend a hand.

'Where is Rob Welton?' Palmer asked.

'Out on the road.'

'Ah — so he intends to pay for his keep.'

'So it appears,' replied Will. He added:

'He is a strange cove and I'm not sure that I like him.'

'Oh and why is that? He seems a sound enough fellow.'

'Rarely does he speak to us. There is something mysterious about him.'

'It's because he has a quiet nature I'm sure.'

'I hope that you're right,' grunted Will. 'But he acts in a queer manner — even if he has a quiet nature as you say.'

'You are too suspicious, Will,' grunted Dick, prodding a large piece of roast buck with his knife. Nothing more was said on the subject and they concentrated upon preparing the evening meal — a meal fit to be consumed by three hungry gentlemen of the road.

The sun had already slipped down behind the trees when the two men sat down around the fire and began eating.

'Did you enjoy yourself this afternoon, Dick?'

'Yes — I met Jeanette Murray.'

Will raised his eyebrows. 'Oh, that surprises me.'

They continued eating. Will asked: 'Did

you find anything? You said you might after inspecting something.'

'So I did,' exclaimed Palmer, a large bone half way to his mouth. 'I forgot all about the matter — I was occupied by other things.'

Will Snell shook his head sadly. 'Ah,' cried he, gazing up in a woeful manner at the blue sky, 'I know not what has become of the youth of today!'

Palmer grinned. 'I shall make a point of looking at the article when next I see her. Then, I hope to have news indeed.'

Will looked at his friend closely. 'It's as well Dick. But remember, the more we know the less safe will we be from the Squire. His desire to get rid of you will be greater than ever.'

'That's true. We must be careful.'

'They only seek you, I think, in a half-hearted manner at present, for nobody misses Simon Beckley.'

'I fancy the Squire will seek me now with greater energy, following my query as to what happened to his first wife,' Palmer observed cheerfully. 'He did not like it at all — as this weal goes to show.'

'Yes, he may think you know more than you do.'

They finished their meal and lay back on the turf. 'Tell me, Dick,' said Will, 'when you have looked at this thing you tell me of — will you know the killer of Simon Beckley?'

'Ah — that I doubt. Mind you, it's only an idea and may prove fruitless, but if it isn't, then we will be much nearer to knowing what exactly goes on in the village.'

Will Snell scratched his forest of red hair. 'Sounds a bit strange to me, but good luck to you,' and the giant picked up the tankard of ale that stood at his side and took a copious draught.

Suddenly the peace of the evening was disturbed by the thud of horses' hoofs and the two men leaped to their feet and looked to their pistols. They need not have troubled, however, for it was Rob Welton returning from the road. He broke through the bushes and dismounted, looking tired and dishevelled.

'Evenin',' greeted Palmer. 'Good hunting?'

For answer Rob Welton produced a large leather purse, up-ended it and a stream of silver coins fell with a merry clink to the ground.

Will's eyes gleamed. 'Now that looks very nice,' said he, suddenly losing his dislike for the lanky highwayman. He gazed with delight upon the pile of coins. 'How do you suggest we share it?'

'As we agreed,' replied Rob, lowering his long frame down beside the fire and ripping off a large piece of meat from the roasted buck. Will Snell nodded and began to deal out the coins between the three of them, counting each one meticulously. Rob Welton glanced over his shoulder. 'Perhaps you should take half,' he suggested, 'seeing that it's you that provides us with our fare.'

'Yes, that's a good idea — I'm all in favour,' commented Palmer.

'As you wish,' cried Will delightedly. He now felt quite friendly towards Welton.

Dick and Will pocketed their share of the spoil and lay back and gazed up into the pale, blue sky, lacerated with long, orange fingers from the setting sun. They relaxed in the peaceful evening silence; dusk was not far distant. The only noise that broke the quietness about them was the hungry munching of Rob Welton by the fire and the stream tumbling down the valley.

Will lighted his pipe and the smoke curled around the den. Dick Palmer lay at ease upon the grass and sniffed the air appreciatively and thought about Jeanette Murray.

11

Rob Welton was quieter than usual at breakfast next morning. He kept his head lowered and his eyes upon his food and all that could be seen was the long narrow scar across his forehead. As he ate, the scar puckered and palpitated as if it were alive.

Will Snell glanced across at him a number of times for he was curious about the man and he often wondered what went on behind that scar. But the tall highwayman gave no indication of what he was thinking about, remaining silent and eating slowly and deliberately. When he had finished he rose and inspected his pistols carefully, and then placed them in his belt and buttoned up his coat.

'I go now upon a special journey,' Rob Welton informed them in a quiet tone. 'You should see the results of it very soon.'

'That's fine,' cried Palmer. 'Happy hunting to you.'

Will Snell made no comment, but stared up thoughtfully at Welton as the man saddled his horse. In a little while the lanky highwayman had completed his preparations and, with a curt nod to his two friends, he mounted and rode slowly out of the den.

'He talks over much,' Wild Will grunted sarcastically.

Dick Palmer nodded. 'Yes, he was very quiet this morning — I wonder what's on his mind?'

Rob Welton reached the edge of the forest and galloped through to the Loughton Road and turned towards the village. He pulled his horse in a little and they slowed to an easy canter. Upon reaching the fork he turned left up the old Epping Road.

It was a dismal morning. The sky was overcast, the air close and heavy, and the whole forest was covered with a dull, lifeless mantle. Welton rode on and in a little while approached the gates of Wake Manor. Here he pulled his horse to a halt and looked quickly up and down the road. Seeing that there was nobody abroad he dug his spurs in and galloped into the drive leading to the Manor.

It was still early morning, but there was a sign of life about the house and grounds. A gardener was bent over a flowerbed beneath one of the windows; an old, white-haired groom led two horses out to the pastures; and a variety of household noises emanated from the Manor. Rob Welton trotted up to the great doors and dismounted, a few paces away from the gardener. The latter, who boasted a straggly, black beard beneath his wizened face, glanced up and stared intently at the newcomer.

'I wish to see the Squire,' announced Welton.

The gardener screwed up one eye and stroked his beard and grinned, showing toothless gums. 'Oh, do 'ee now — and 'oo might you be?'

'Never mind who I am — I wish to see the Squire at once on important business.'

The old man was not impressed however, and he remained standing where he was, half bent, gazing saucily up at the highwayman. Realising that he was wasting his time with the fellow, Welton turned and strode up the steps and knocked loudly on the big doors. The gardener watched with interest. At last one door opened and a liveried footman appeared.

'I wish to speak with the Squire,' said Welton.

The footman raised an eyebrow and stared at him in a lofty manner. 'The Squire, villager, is busy.'

'Tell him,' said Welton between his teeth, for he found the fellow exasperating. 'I have news which will be of great interest to him.'

'Can you not tell me?'

Rob Welton glanced contemptuously at the footman. 'What I have to say is for his ears only. Now come, man, announce me. It's important.'

The footman hesitated, shrugged his shoulders, and then withdrew in an unhurried manner. He crossed the hall and disappeared through a door on the far side. Rob Welton turned and, ignoring the curious old man, stared about the grounds of Wake Manor. The gardener, still standing half bent over the flowerbed, eyed him inquisitively. Footsteps sounded in the hall again and Welton turned back to see a tall, dark, immaculately dressed man approaching. It was the Squire. Rob Welton touched his hat and gave a slight bow.

'Well, man, what have you to say?' asked the Squire impatiently.

The highwayman glanced around at the gardener, who was now deeply engrossed in his task of weeding the flowerbed. 'What I have to say,' replied Welton coolly 'is for your ears only.'

Adam Penfield glanced quickly at the old gardener and then back at Welton. He seemed undecided. The highwayman's confident manner, however, intrigued the Squire. At last he beckoned Welton to follow him and then swung about and reentered the house. He crossed the hall, the highwayman close behind, and opened a door at the side of the staircase. They entered and the Squire closed the door quietly behind them. Welton found himself in a small, plainly furnished study and from the stale, dusty smell that hung about, it was obviously not in use.

'Well? What is your name?' snapped the Squire, 'and what have you to tell me?'

'My name,' said the highwayman, 'is Rob Welton. What I have to tell you is this — I know where the highwayman Dick Palmer is.'

'Dick Palmer?' frowned the Squire. 'Who may he be?'

Rob Welton took a deep breath and his thoughts tumbled quickly over one another. Could it be that he had made a mistake? His heart beat rapidly, then suddenly he realised that Palmer might not have given his proper name when he was captured.

'Do you not know Dick Palmer — the son of Dick Turpin — the man you had put in prison, but who escaped?'

The Squire's eyes gleamed. 'Ah — yes, yes. So — you know where he is?'

Rob Welton leaned leisurely up against the small table in the middle of the room and stared at the Squire speculatively. 'Yes. Do you wish to know?'

'I do, but one moment. Why so willing,

my friend, to tell me?'

'I have my reasons,' replied Welton, smiling slightly, 'and I know you wish him out of the way.'

The Squire's eyes narrowed and he remained very still, then he began rubbing his cheek with one, slim finger. 'How do you know that?' he asked carefully.

'Never mind, it's sufficient that I do. You wish to know his whereabouts or not?'

'Yes,' replied Penfield, then added: 'I take it you have no particular love for him?'

Rob Welton ignored the question. 'I shall have to show you the way to his hideout. It is not easy to find.'

Adam Penfield stared down at the floor and did not answer. He began stroking his cheek again and then, deep in thought, he started walking up and down the room. Welton remained by the table, watching him. Suddenly the Squire stopped and turned round.

'Do you know a girl by the name of Jeanette Murray?' he asked abruptly.

Rob Welton was taken by surprise. He hesitated, but he could not see any trick in the question. 'I know of her,' he replied warily. 'She is Palmer's lover.'

The Squire gave a start. 'What!' he exclaimed. 'Palmer's lover?' He stepped quickly forward and grasped Welton's arms. 'Is that true?'

'I am certain of it,' grunted Welton, moving out of Penfield's grasp.

'Well, well, well,' murmured the Squire, smiling broadly, 'that is most interesting.' He turned away and stood with his back to the highwayman, thinking deeply. At last he faced his visitor again.

'Matters are simplified,' he said. 'Listen, my friend — you dislike, you say, the son of Dick Turpin. Therefore I gather you would not mind causing him some little bother before capturing him?' The Squire leaned forward, his dark yes gleaming brightly.

Rob Welton did not reply, but waited for the Squire to explain himself further. The highwayman was not feeling so sure of his ground now and one hand rested upon one of the pistols beneath his coat.

The Squire continued. 'I wish to speak to her — speak to this girl, Jeanette Murray, alone at the Manor here.' He paused and smiled amiably. 'However,' he went on, 'it is rather awkward to reach her, but if you know her lover — this man Palmer — then perhaps you could assist me?'

The Squire waited patiently for an answer, watching Rob Welton closely. There was a short silence in the room. The highwayman wanted to make quite sure he was not stepping into a trap, for he was uncertain of the Squire's game. But he still had a trump card — he would have to take a chance.

'I think I might — it would suit me very well,' he said.

'Good,' exclaimed the Squire. 'However, one other thing — how do I know I can trust you?'

Welton smiled. 'You do not, but would I have come here and offered you my services otherwise?'

'That is true,' agreed the Squire.

'For that matter — how do I know that I can trust you?'

Adam Penfield gave a low laugh. 'That also is true!'

'At any rate that does not concern me,' commented Welton. He stopped and stared steadily at the Squire and then he added in a soft voice: 'I know too much about you Squire, for it to be worth your while to double-cross me, for some foolish reason.'

Penfield's face blanched and he glared at Welton searchingly, and fear clutched at his heart. He saw that his visitor was not bluffing. 'What do you mean?' he asked.

'It's of no moment. What do you wish me to do? I think your scheme an excellent one.' And then quite abruptly the highwayman's scar on his forehead turned deep red and the skin around it creased and grew taut. 'It will give me infinite pleasure, my dear Squire,' he hissed, 'to watch Palmer grow crazy with worry before he dies!'

Adam Penfield noted the sudden change with interest and his brain worked rapidly and a triumphant gleam entered his eyes. At last, he mused, his objective was in sight. When next he spoke he had decided upon his plan of action.

'Go to the girl and tell her Palmer has met with an accident — has been injured,' he said deliberately. 'Does she know you?'

'No,' replied Welton, 'but Palmer may have mentioned my name to her. In any case I know enough about their little romance to convince her I know him.'

'Fine. Get her and bring her here — I don't mind how you do it. One other thing — make absolutely sure she is wearing a ring upon her right hand.'

Rob Welton nodded. 'I understand. I will do that with pleasure. When?'

'Let me see. Tomorrow — tomorrow night,' Penfield told him.

'As you wish — and what about Palmer?'

'We can take him afterwards. He will be no trouble — it will be a surprise. You wilt receive your entertainment then — with both of them here.'

Rob Welton nodded and watched the Squire with some curiosity, for the man was obviously greatly pleased with the arrangements, in fact he seemed highly excited. His eyes glittered with triumph and his slim but powerful hands clenched and unclenched with nervous anticipation. The lanky highwayman wondered why he wanted the girl so much. But Welton, himself, was well satisfied with matters and he looked forward to the time when he would be able to watch the expression on Dick Palmer's face when he heard his beloved Jeanette was in the hands of Adam Penfield. The big highwayman grinned to himself and then, looking up, he saw that the Squire was eyeing him in a most unpleasant fashion. The look disappeared immediately.

'You will not fail me?' the Squire asked.

'Why should I?' replied Welton. 'As you have gathered I don't like our friend Dick Palmer. The taking of his woman will not please him — thus I am as keen as you.'

'Keen as me, eh?' murmured Penfield, and he suddenly began laughing and his laughter rose higher and higher until it echoed shrilly about the room. Then it gradually faded away again to a low chuckle. 'Keen as me, eh?' he reiterated, 'that is funny,' and he gurgled away cheerfully to himself for several minutes. He stared at Welton, smoothed his dark wig carefully with one hand, and asked in a light-hearted manner: 'Tell me, my friend, what is this stupid gossip that you have heard about me?'

Rob Welton was not fooled, however, by his casual manner. 'One name it is sufficient to mention,' he said very quietly watching the Squire's face. 'Louisa Martilliére!'

Adam Penfield drew in his breath quickly and stepped back a pace as if evading a blow. His face suddenly turned livid and his dark eyes narrowed to mere pinpoints, his smooth forehead creasing and wrinkling in a terrible manner. Welton watched this transformation in amazement and he suddenly realised with what kind of man he was faced, but the expression was gone as swiftly as it had come and the highwayman was wondering whether he had been seeing things.

'Well, well,' said the Squire evenly. 'Never mind. You will carry out this little plan of ours, will you not?'

'Your private affairs are of no interest to me, sir,' replied Welton quietly.

'Of course not,' said the Squire affably. 'Good. Then I can expect to see you tomorrow night?'

'You can — with the girl.'

Adam Penfield rubbed his hands. 'I will await you,' he said and then he crossed the room and opened the door. Welton followed him out across the hall. The Squire opened the big doors and the highwayman strode down the steps.

'Pleasant journeying,' Penfield called to him.

Welton did not answer, but mounted his horse and with a curt nod, rode off down the drive. After the highwayman had disappeared around the corner the Squire remained standing on the steps of the Manor for some time, staring thoughtfully towards the forest. His face was expressionless, but in his dark eyes there was an exultant gleam. At last, still deep in thought, he stepped back and closed the doors and made his way across the hall to the rear of the house.

Welton broke into a gallop when he

reached the highway for he did not wish to be too long away from the hideout. He must keep a careful watch on Palmer's movements and arrange his trip to the Black Horse Inn when the young highwayman was occupied at the cave. He reached the road junction and turned right. His thoughts centred on Adam Penfield and a look of distaste entered his eyes. The Squire was not a pleasant person to know, that was obvious, and the highwayman knew perfectly well that once he had handed over the girl his life would not be worth a silver coin. He would have to take great care. Welton smiled then at the thought of the way in which Adam Penfield would treat the girl and of Dick Palmer's reaction at the news. This put him in quite a pleasant mood and he approached the den with a cheerful grin on his thin face.

Will Snell was giving his black stallion a rub down when Welton entered the hideout. 'So you're back,' commented Will. 'Any luck?'

'No, not this time — cannot always be lucky.'

'That's true,' replied Wild Will, fingering his wiry beard. 'It's all part of the great game — you have good luck and you have bad. The thing to remember is if you had nothing but good luck then there'd be no call to play the game of High Toby — an' if that were so, then it would be a sad thing indeed!'

To this Rob Welton had no answer and he unsaddled his horse and sat down by the fire. Dick Palmer appeared at the mouth of the cave carrying a large pie, which Will Snell had procured from a source he refused to divulge, only that morning. 'Come, me hearties,' cried Dick, 'it's time to fill our bellies again.'

Over the meal Dick and Will decided to try their hand that afternoon upon the Great North Road. After the repast they rested and then some time later, greatly refreshed, they saddled their steeds and set out, leaving Rob Welton asleep by the side of the fire. In an hour or so they at last reached the great highway and, hiding themselves behind a large, spreading oak tree, they adjusted their masks and settled down to await the coming of a suitable prey. Their pistols were cocked ready in their hands.

Some time passed by and no traveller appeared. Will was about to mutter to his friend that their luck was out when there came the sound of the distant clatter of horses' hoofs. In a few moments round the farthest bend rode two horsemen. They rode leisurely and their loud, cheerful conversation reached the ears of the two men in the shadows beneath the oak tree. Will and Dick waited until they were almost abreast and then, spurring forward they charged out abruptly in front of the unsuspecting travellers.

'Avast,' roared Will, 'your money or your lives!'

The two plump travellers gasped with fear and hastily pulled their horses to a halt.

'Mercy, mercy,' cried one, 'do not shoot!'

'Villains,' roared the other, 'you will be hanged for this — don't you know who I am?'

'Pardon my ignorance,' replied Will humbly, 'but I cannot say that I do.'

'I, foolish rogues, am Sir Patrick Hamilton.'

'Pleasant afternoon to you, sir,' said Will affably. Then in a grimmer tone: 'Now, quick, hand over your valuables!'

Sir Patrick gasped with horror and he began expostulating and waving his arms about in a most weird manner.

'Come, Hamilton,' cried his companion, 'can't you see these fellows mean business — let's hand over our money and be rid of them.'

'It's outrageous,' shouted the knight. He stared unbelievingly at the two highwaymen, then suddenly he quieted down for he saw that they did indeed mean business. Unwillingly he threw his heavy purse across to Dick Palmer's outstretched hands. Palmer thereupon stowed it away with the one he had already collected from Hamilton's companion.

'Now be off with you!' cried Will Snell.

Sir Patrick Hamilton's flabby countenance turned deep red, and he looked as if he were about to explode at such impudence, but somehow he restrained himself and, gathering his reins in his hands, he spurred forward again, closely followed by his companion. When he had ridden thirty paces the knight looked back over his shoulder. 'Villainous rogues,' he screamed.

Laughter, however, followed him up the road; then Dick Palmer and Will Snell, highly elated at the success of their expedition, turned their horses round, broke through the bushes into the forest and set off on the long journey back to the cave.

12

The following day the sky hung grey and ominous over Epping Forest and in the early afternoon the light began to wane and grow feeble. Behind the forest to the east a yellow glow appeared.

The three highwaymen sat around the fire gazing silently into the embers. Will Snell glanced up at the grey sky and grunted: 'We are in for a mighty storm.'

Dick Palmer nodded. 'Yes. It has been building up to it these past two days, and I can see myself getting wet.'

'Ah, of course — you are going on that trip of yours,' murmured Will, glancing quickly at his friend. 'Hope you're successful.'

Welton yawned. 'It's an inauspicious time you pick, Dick,' he said. 'You'll return like a wet dog.'

Will Snell glanced with some surprise at their lanky companion, for it seemed that his tongue was at last loosening. But

Welton's face was expressionless and, though he knew the giant was observing him, he remained staring into the fire.

'I am not bothered,' Palmer remarked. He got to his feet and stepped over to Red Ruby. The chestnut mare was acting a little restlessly, for she knew well enough that a storm was in the offing. 'Now, now, take it easy old girl,' Dick murmured, patting her red mane. 'Surely you don't mind a little rain?'

Rob Welton suddenly turned round and glanced across at Palmer. 'I expect you will be back for tea, eh?' he asked abruptly, giving a little self-conscious laugh.

Palmer stared at him in surprise and Will Snell looked up in astonishment. It was the first time a personal question — even one as paltry as this — had been asked on either side. Of what interest could it be to Rob Welton to know when Dick Palmer would return? A short silence followed the unexpected query.

'Yes, I think I will be,' Dick replied at last, in a quiet tone.

Welton quickly turned back to the fire

again and lowered his eyes and his face went a little red. Dick Palmer remained standing by the side of his horse staring at Rob Welton's back, and for the first time a feeling of uncertainty towards the man entered his mind. The question had absolutely startled Wild Will and now all his previous distrust for Welton flooded back and he gazed at the tall highwayman with open hostility in his eyes. Welton, on his part, remained quiet with his head lowered.

Dick Palmer mounted Red Ruby and rode softly out of the den and not a further word was spoken. Palmer tried hard to believe there was a simple, innocent reason for Welton's question, but the way in which the highwayman had tried to laugh it off did not seem right. Dick came to the reluctant conclusion that some evil purpose prompted the question. But what? He had no idea. His thoughts upon this subject, however, soon faded, for he was approaching the Black Horse Inn.

Palmer dismounted behind the stables and tethered Red Ruby to a tree. He stepped forward cautiously and looked quickly around the yard. It was empty. He could see no one in the kitchen. Abruptly he darted forward across the yard; reaching the kitchen door, he knocked softly. Immediately he heard the sound of light footsteps crossing the kitchen floor and then the door opened. It was Jeanette herself. She gasped surprise and stepped back a pace.

'I must see you at once,' Dick murmured urgently. 'Where can we go?'

She came outside and closed the door softly behind her. 'It's safest in the forest,' she replied swiftly. 'What is the matter?'

Dick Palmer did not reply but, catching her hand, he led her across the yard. As they passed the stables the highwayman saw Nicholas Wilken at work in his tiny room. The ostler saw them and waved cheerily and Jeanette waved back with a smile. Palmer led the way through the trees towards the hollow that they had frequented before. Directly they arrived there, Jeanette turned to him with an anxious frown.

'Now what is amiss?' she cried.

He grasped her right hand and gazed down at the ring she wore. 'Take your ring off,' he said. 'Only an idea, but it may bear fruit.'

She stared at Dick in surprise, but withdrew the ring from her slim finger and handed it to him. Palmer stared at it closely, turning it this way and that. The mounting, which held a single, glittering stone, was oval in shape and of unusual depth and seemed out of proportion with the rest of the ring.

'Why such a large mounting?' Dick asked her. 'It's ugly. This is the ring they found upon you in the cradle, isn't it?'

'Yes,' said she. 'Why do you ask?'

The highwayman did not reply, but continued to inspect the ring very closely. He turned it upside down and looked inside beneath the mounting. Jeannette watched him curiously, a puzzled frown upon her forehead.

'Aha!' cried Palmer suddenly.

'What is it?' she asked eagerly.

Dick's eyes shone triumphantly. 'Look at that,' he cried. 'Look at that!'

Jeannette bent forward and then was

able to see that inside the ring on the bottom of the mounting there was a tiny hole. Surrounding it there was some intricate flowered tracery. The girl stared at the hole blankly and then looked up at Dick. 'What about it?'

'Have you a pin?' cried Palmer excitedly.

She produced one, and the highwayman took it carefully and holding the ring upside down, he stuck the point into the tiny hole. He pressed down hard and, without warning, the top of the mounting holding the stone flew back, revealing beneath a small cavity! The couple stared, wide-eyed, into the opening. Lying at the bottom was a tiny piece of folded paper. Palmer dipped in one finger, trying to pull it out, but he could not reach it — his finger was too big.

'Here, you try,' he cried to Jeanette.

She put her slim finger into the cavity, caught the bit of paper with her nail and scooped it out. It fell from her finger and dropped to the ground. Dick bent hastily and retrieved it. With a beating heart he unfolded the tiny piece of paper, then he smoothed it out on the palm of his hand.

'It's a birth certificate!' Jeannette gasped.

Palmer nodded slowly and then he began reading out what was written on the certificate. *I, the undersigned, do certify that the Birth of Jeanette Martilliére Penfield born on the 23rd day of April, one thousand, seven hundred and thirty hath been —* ' Dick trailed off and gazed at the girl. Jeanette herself was staring down at the paper stupefied, her eyes glued to it. She shook her head in a dazed manner.

'I must sit down,' she murmured.

They seated themselves on the bank and stared down at the piece of paper in Dick Palmer's hand. At last Jeanette spoke. 'So — So Squire Penfield is my father!'

Palmer lay back on the bank and scratched his head. 'Yes, I am afraid so,' he replied.

She looked at him quickly, noting his tone of voice. 'You suspected it then?' she cried.

Palmer nodded. 'I thought something of the sort might be the case,' he said. 'By all accounts your mother — she was French you know — was a very beautiful woman — like you, I expect. She, too, had black hair.'

Again there was silence, and in the forest around them there was silence too, for black, threatening clouds hung across the skies and the birds and beasts lay in fear of the impending storm.

'I have been celebrating my birthday on the wrong day,' Jeanette murmured inconsequently.

'It seems you were born in Marylebone,' said Dick. He folded up the certificate and replaced it in the cavity in the mounting and handed it back to the girl.

'I must think,' he grunted, gazing up into the trees.

'What shall I do?' Jeanette cried helplessly.

'The motive is now a little clearer,' Palmer commented, half to himself.

'What — what is the motive? I cannot see it,'

'I imagine he seeks something of value, but you, for some reason, are in the way. If he can obtain your birth certificate, then you could never prove that you are his daughter.'

'Oh,' gasped Jeanette, 'I see. But surely he has more right to whatever he seeks than I?'

'One would think so, but it can't be the case. However — we must not jump to conclusions for we don't know everything yet.'

'How came I to be in a cradle in the forest?'

'That I know not either, but this discovery has cleared up many things — the mysterious searching of your rooms and the attacks, for instance.'

They were silent for a little while. The news that she was the real daughter of Adam Penfield, Squire of Wake Manor, came, naturally enough, as a shock to Jeanette and for several minutes she sat quietly by herself, trying to collect her thoughts, trying to understand what it all meant. Her finely moulded features lay in repose as she gazed thoughtfully across the glade, the long, black, silky tresses of her hair framing her face and making a lovely picture. Dick Palmer was content to sit by her side and gaze upon her great beauty. In a little while the excitement, which had followed the discovery of the birth certificate, died away and they could now face the problem with calm, clear minds.

Jeanette moved closer to Dick and grasped his hand. 'What shall we do?' she asked.

Palmer shook his head. 'I am not sure,' he replied slowly.

'Shall we tell Constable Pucky and see what he can do?'

'Of what use would he be? All we are able to prove is that you are Penfield's daughter — naught else.'

Jeanette gave a pretty shrug to her shoulders.

'It would serve no purpose,' Dick Palmer continued. 'In fact you would be in great danger. The Squire it seems has no right to whatever he seeks whilst you are alive, but — ' Palmer did not finish his sentence.

Jeanette gasped for she knew what he meant. 'Yes,' she breathed, 'you are right — directly he knew that his secret was out, his only chance would be to — to kill me!'

Palmer put his arm around her shoulders. 'He will not do that,' he said quietly, 'whilst I'm alive.'

She snuggled close to him and rested her head upon his chest. 'What shall we do?' she asked again, content to leave the matter in his hands.

'We must take a bold step,' Palmer replied. 'Remember — your mother died mysteriously and there is the untimely demise of Simon Beckley when he was about to speak of the Squire. We have been making wild guesses — we don't know the whole story yet.'

'I will never let the wicked Squire — my father — take anything that should be mine,' cried Jeanette in a resolute tone. 'What's our next step?'

'I must think over the matter. But we cannot afford to be idle any longer. It's too dangerous for you.'

'I do not mind,' said she. Dick Palmer lifted her up and their lips met and they clung to each other.

'I must go now,' Palmer whispered. 'I'll

ride over this evening with a solution. Do not tell your parents until I arrive.'

'As you wish,' she replied, and she rose and made her way back to the inn.

'Wait!' Dick called. She stopped and looked back. Palmer hurried after her. 'I think it would be best that I take your birth certificate.'

She nodded and took off her ring again. Dick pressed the mounting and withdrew the paper and then handed the ring back. He tucked the certificate carefully away in his coat pocket. 'Until this evening, then,' he cried cheerfully.

Jeanette smiled. 'Until this evening,' she replied, and then she ran quickly back to the inn.

The highwayman waited until he saw her enter then he returned to Red Ruby, mounted and spurred the mare through the forest at a great pace. In a short time he was slithering down the slope towards the thicket hiding the cave. He broke through and dismounted hastily and then noted with chagrin that Rob Welton was still there — he had wanted to discuss the latest development with Will Snell.

Realising he would have to wait until Welton left the hideout, Palmer tied his mare to the pole and joined the others by the fire.

Wild Will glanced up at him and nodded, and the giant saw by his young friend's expression that he had news of some importance to impart. The air between the three of them soon became tense and Rob Welton, sensing it, suddenly rose and stretched himself.

'I think I'll take a ride abroad,' he said.

There was no answer and Palmer waited impatiently whilst Welton leisurely prepared his steed. At last, however, the tall highwayman was mounted and in a few moments had ridden away.

'It's as I thought,' Dick cried to Will. 'She is the daughter of Adam Penfield — her ring contained her birth certificate.'

Will Snell's jaw promptly dropped open and he stared at his friend incredulously. Palmer quickly outlined the position to him and Will listened intently.

'So,' Dick ended, 'something must be done immediately, for it is obvious the

Squire will try to obtain it again, and who knows what might happen this time.'

Will Snell nodded slowly. He picked up a smouldering stick and stared thoughtfully at the glowing end. 'Let me think a moment,' he murmured. Palmer waited patiently whilst Will scrutinised the stick with apparent keen interest. At last he turned and faced his friend.

'Yes Dick, you are right. Speed is essential. The case has come to a merry pass. Here's an idea — it's a gamble, but I think it's the best way. We must confront the Squire with what we know and see what becomes of it!'

'Ah — that is what I had thought too.'

'The girl is in danger, there's no doubt about that. We must act with all possible haste.'

'Good,' cried Dick. 'You have spoken my thoughts. This is what I suggest, but first let us go to the Black Horse Inn, Chief Constable, or no, for Jeanette must be guarded. There we can lay our plans over a pint of their excellent ale, and we can inform Jeanette then of what we intend to do.'

'A fine idea, Dick. Come, see to your pistols and then let us get off.'

The two highwaymen jumped to their feet and in a short while they were mounted, armed to the teeth. They burst out of the glade and galloped up the valley, not long after Rob Welton. As they entered the forest a strong wind suddenly blew up and whistled and roared through the trees like a live thing.

'Alas,' cried Will, 'the storm is upon us.' And all at once the rain swept down upon them and lashed across their backs.

Heedless of the storm's fury they rode on towards the village, bent low in their saddles, peering ahead through the dusk and stinging rain. They reached the highway and spurred on towards High Beach, little guessing that Rob Welton's destination was the same and that the tall highwayman had already arrived at the Black Horse Inn.

13

Rob Welton rode swiftly through the trees after leaving the cave and passed round the village green, taking the same route as that often taken by Dick Palmer. He knew from what he had heard Palmer say, that by this route he could approach the Black Horse Inn from the rear with little chance of being observed. He had already decided upon the tale he would tell the girl and he smiled to himself as he passed the village church, for he thought the Squire's scheme an excellent one.

Soon he reached the back of the inn and dismounted, having ridden as near as he dare. He glanced up into the lighted room of the ostler and saw that the youth was deeply engrossed in the task of repairing a saddle. Welton stepped noiselessly across the stable yard and reached the wall of the inn near the kitchen window. Leaning forward he glanced in and then smiled triumphantly. Jeanette

Murray was washing up in the kitchen by herself and thus it was she that would most likely answer the door. It was better so, for if the landlord met the highwayman he might smell a rat.

Creeping back to the door Welton gave a light tap. The sound of clinking crockery inside the kitchen ceased and a short silence followed. The highwayman only hoped she did not call her father. Then quick footsteps crossed the kitchen and a second later the door opened. The girl peered out cautiously and stared questioningly at the tall, lean man that stood on the doorstep in the dim evening light.

'My name is Rob Welton,' the highwayman murmured hurriedly, a worried frown upon his forehead.

Jeanette gasped and swung the door open wide. 'What is it?' she said in a hushed whisper, fear entering her eyes. 'What is the matter?'

'It's about Dick Palmer,' Welton said hesitantly.

'What? Oh dear — what has happened?'

'I am his friend you know, I — '

'Yes, he told me about you.'

'Well er — Constable Pucky met him — on the way back to the cave.' Welton took a deep breath. 'He — he shot him!'

Jeanette's dark eyes opened wide and her hands flew to her lips, holding back the scream that sprang to her throat. The expression on her face asked him to go on.

'I am afraid he is sorely wounded — he calls for you.'

Jeanette gave a little cry of anguish and she stared almost unbelievingly at Welton for several moments, hoping that somehow he had made a mistake. But the highwayman's sad, awkward look was convincing enough.

'Oh dear,' she breathed and then abruptly her manner changed. 'Wait — wait one moment,' she commanded. 'Let me fetch my cloak and I will be with you.'

Welton stepped forward and murmured swiftly: 'It would be best to keep the matter secret.'

Jeanette nodded quickly. 'Yes, yes — I will tell no one. My parents are busy in the bar — please wait one moment and I will join you.'

She stepped back into the kitchen and hurried across to the parlour and collected her cloak. Welton waited somewhat nervously, glancing this way and that, fearing that they might be disturbed at the crucial moment. Nicholas Wilken was still in his little room above the stable intent upon his work.

Jeanette reappeared at the door clad in her cardinal. Rob Welton remembered at that moment that the Squire had told him to make sure the girl wore the ring. Quickly he glanced down at her hand, then sighed with relief — yes, she wore a large ring upon the second finger of her right hand.

'How do we travel?' the girl asked.

'My horse is sturdy,' the highwayman told her, 'she can carry two. It will be best — we must not disturb the village.'

'No, no, of course not — lead the way to your steed then, and take care — the ostler is in his room.'

Rob Welton nodded, turned about and walked quietly back across the yard followed by the girl. As they passed close to the stable wall Jeanette caught her foot against a stone and immediately they heard the ostler above rise and approach the window. The highwayman and the girl huddled close to the wall scarcely breathing. Wilken gazed out into the night, trying to see what had disturbed him. At last he was satisfied that nothing was amiss and he returned to his seat. The couple below sighed with relief and crept forward again to the forest at the back. The highwayman reached his horse and mounted and then he leaned down and lifted Jeanette up behind him. Jeanette sat side-saddle for she wore a long dress. Without a word Rob Welton touched the horse's flanks and they set off slowly through the forest.

Welton rode due north from the inn so as to cut through the forest to the old Epping Road — and Wake Manor. They had not travelled far when the storm came upon them and they must needs bend almost double to protect themselves against the stinging drops. Jeanette glanced up once or twice and looked about her, but the sheets of rain that swept across their path obscured any forest landmarks that she might know and so she bent her head again, relying on the man in front to find his way to the cave of Dick Palmer.

At last they reached the Epping Road and such was the fury of the storm that the girl was still unable to pick out any of the landmarks — to realise that this was not the Loughton Road. Not until they actually rode in at the gates of Wake Manor did it dawn upon her that things were not as they should be.

'Where are we?' she called.

The highwayman did not answer.

And then it was that Jeanette recognised the drive of Wake Manor and suddenly fear clutched at her heart. 'Where are you taking me?' she cried.

Still there was no answer.

The girl now grew terrified and she thumped the highwayman's back with all her might, screaming to him to stop, but Rob Welton heeded her not. Jeanette's terror increased and she became hysterical and cried out wildly to the man in front of her to set her down and release her, but it was of no use — he just ignored the girl. She hit him with all her strength, but Welton leaned forward in the saddle and the blows had little effect upon him.

'Stop, stop — please stop — release me!' the girl cried. Her cloak had come undone, the rain lashed upon her thin dress and her black hair waved in the wind, so that she presented a pitiful sight.

They rode up to the front of the Manor and Jeanette, looking fearfully towards the sombre house, saw Adam Penfield standing motionless in the great doorway, silhouetted against the light from the hall behind. The Squire had heard her screams and had come out to meet them and assist Rob Welton to carry the girl inside.

★　★　★

It was at about this time that Dick Palmer and Will Snell rode up to the front of the Black Horse Inn. They handed their steeds to Nicholas Wilken, who stared open-mouthed at the huge Will Snell, and then strode audaciously into the inn.

There were three villagers inside the bar room and the squat form of Harry Murray was behind the bar. The landlord saw Dick Palmer at once and gazed at him in amazement. The highwayman beckoned him and Murray hurried over.

'This is madness, Dick,' he whispered, directly he reached them. 'The Chief Constable is in the village at this very moment.'

Dick Palmer shrugged. 'Is the little room at the back occupied?' he asked. 'My friend and I wish to drink and converse without being disturbed.'

'No, it is not. Come, I will take you there.'

The landlord hurried out of the bar and down the passage, seeming more relieved than the two highwaymen that the three villagers had paid them scant attention. Harry turned the corner at the end and opened the door and ushered Dick and Will inside — into the room in which Simon Beckley had met his end.

'I will bring you a quart of ale each,' whispered the landlord, and he departed on his errand.

'This is the place, Will,' Dick exclaimed. 'The shot, I reckon, came through that window — and he fell forward over this table here. Look — the wood is still marked with his blood.'

'I see,' grunted Will. The great fellow stepped to the window and glanced out. He gazed thoughtfully about the yard. 'It would be an easy matter, Dick; for an agile fellow to climb yonder stable roof and fire from there, but he would need to be an accurate shot.'

'Why, yes,' cried Dick, hurrying over to the window. 'I think you have something there, Will.'

They returned to the table and sat down, and in a few moments Harry Murray appeared again carrying two huge tankards of ale. Will Snell slapped his lips and Dick Palmer delved into his coat pocket for a coin. The landlord held up his hand.

'No, Dick, it's my pleasure. The debt I owe you can never be fully repaid, but

I can provide you with free ale!'

Will Snell's large blue eyes nearly fell out.

'Well, well — that is very kind of you, Harry,' Dick replied with great delight. 'Then our toast must be to you.' The two highwaymen raised their tankards and drank deeply.

'I am going to enjoy this night,' cried Will, wiping his mouth with the back of his hairy hand.

'Ring the bell when you require me,' Harry Murray said, 'and I will bring more.' He nodded cordially and went out.

Will Snell and Dick Palmer smiled happily at each other and settled down to work out their plan of campaign and to drink the health of the landlord of the Black Horse Inn.

★   ★   ★

Rob Welton jumped down from his horse and told the girl to dismount. This she did as best she could without his assistance and the highwayman then grasped her arm and dragged her up the steps before the Squire. Penfield clutched the girl and glanced quickly at her right hand.

'You have done well, my friend,' he cried to Welton. 'Come inside and I will repay you.'

Rob Welton gave a slight smile and stepped quickly back to his horse. 'Don't worry yourself, Squire — I need none of it.' And, before Penfield could stop him, Welton had mounted his steed again and was galloping like the wind down the drive. The Squire watched him go with a frown, then he shrugged his shoulders and turned and led the girl into the house. Jeanette, glad to take shelter from the storm and feeling very weary, went meekly with him.

Welton rode at a tremendous pace back towards the village to make sure of his escape, for, if the truth be known, he greatly feared the Squire of Wake Manor. He dismounted at the inn and went inside and made his way towards the little room at the back, where he knew he could have a quiet drink by himself. He turned the corner and opened the door — then stopped dead in his tracks at sight of the two occupants.

The three men stared at one another in bewilderment. Dick Palmer was equal to the occasion, however, and, after a second or so of hesitation, he jumped to his feet.

'Well — well — well, Rob, and it's you! We did not quite expect you, but come on in and join us in a drink!'

Realising that he had no alternative but to accept the invitation, Welton gave a somewhat feeble smile and joined them at the table. Will Snell, with a dubious look, rang the bell for Harry Murray. That worthy soon appeared at the door, crying: 'Not another one surely, Will?'

'No, not this time, Harry,' grunted Will, with a slight slur to his speech. 'It's for our friend here who has this moment arrived — from nowhere it seems.'

'I see,' replied the landlord vaguely. 'I will bring him a tankard this very moment, and whilst I'm at it you'd better have another one. My legs are getting tired running to and fro trying to quench your eternal thirst!' With that the landlord hurried off.

Adam Penfield took Jeanette into the room at the front of the manor, and as she entered the girl saw the Squire's wife, Charlotte, sitting on a settee by the window. Jeanette noticed the high hair-do towering above the woman's heavily painted face and her rich, flowing petticoats. The two women stared straight at each other and Jeanette took an instant dislike to the Squire's wife.

'Your ring,' demanded the Squire, holding out his hand.

Jeanette, knowing the little casket to be empty, handed it over without a word. The girl had not spoken at all since she had arrived but she had lost her fear now.

Charlotte Penfield instinctively knew what Jeanette thought of them and she rose from the settee with some effort and walked slowly across to the girl, her skirts swishing on the floor. She stopped in front of her and they glared defiantly at one another and suddenly the elder woman, her painted face reddening with fury at Jeanette's scornful expression, lifted her hand and dealt the girl a violent blow on the side of her face. Jeanette gave a low gasp and was about to strike the woman back when she realised the foolhardiness of such an act with Adam Penfield present, and gritting her teeth she remained still.

The Squire's wife turned and swayed jauntily back to her seat. Abruptly there came a cry from the Squire, who had been intent upon the ring and had hardly noticed the incident between the two women.

'It is empty — it is empty!' he screamed, staring down into the tiny opening in the ring.

'What!' cried Charlotte Penfield, and she scrambled to her feet again and hurried across to her husband's side.

The Squire glanced up at Jeanette. 'Where is it?' he snapped, a terrible glint in his dark eyes.

'Where is what?' asked the girl innocently.

Penfield hesitated and stared at Jeanette searchingly for several moments. Abruptly he turned to his wife. 'It's no matter,' he whispered. 'It would have made things easier, but I think she knows who she really is; it will be sufficient for her to sign the paper with two of my men as witnesses.'

The Squire thereupon delved into his waistcoat pocket and, with a flourish, produced a large piece of paper. This he unfolded with great care, then stepped over to the girl and handed it to her.

'Sign this with your correct name,' he said quietly, 'and all will be well.'

Jeanette, filled with curiosity, took the paper and moved under the chandelier to read it the better. Adam Penfield and his wife watched her closely and the suppressed excitement that characterised their demeanour at that moment did not escape the girl, and she began reading the document with some interest.

Silence filled the room, broken only by the lashing of the rain upon the windows and the far-off deep roaring of the gale as it rampaged through the forest. This is what Jeanette Murray read:-

I hereby bequeath the Martilliére family jewels and heirlooms, inherited by me upon the death of my mother, Louisa Penfield (nee Martilliére), who herself had them settled upon her for life and on death to her daughter absolutely, to my father, Adam Penfield, of Wake Manor, High Beach, Essex.

Signed: July 1750.

Jeanette's thoughts tumbled over one another. So that is what it was all about! She would have to be very careful if she wished to escape from the situation. Of course she would not sign it. She looked up: 'You wish me to sign this with my name — Jeanette Murray?' she asked coolly.

The Squire pursed his lips. 'Come, girl, no foolishness, please — with your real name; you know it.'

'I am afraid I don't know what you are talking about.'

Adam Penfield cursed between his teeth. He strode across the room and, without giving any indication of his intention, struck Jeanette a savage blow on the side of her face. The girl staggered back, holding one hand to her cheek, suddenly tripped and fell headlong to the floor. She remained there in a dazed condition.

'Sign it!' roared Penfield. 'Sign it with your proper name — Jeanette Martilliére Penfield!'

Jeanette blinked up at him through the tears that welled from her eyes, then she struggled to her feet, crossed the room and collapsed on a chair. She felt the bruise on her cheek tenderly and quite abruptly she became filled with self-pity. Then, as abruptly again, a fierce hatred filled her and she gazed across at the fiend that was her father and stubbornly resolved never to sign the document.

'I refuse to!' she cried out.

'Let me deal with her,' said Charlotte Penfield, sweeping across the room. She grasped Jeanette roughly and began slapping the girl's head from side to side. Jeanette leaped to her feet again and, escaping from the elder woman's grip, dealt Charlotte a hard blow in the middle of her face. Fiercely they began fighting, but Jeanette was no match for the heavier built woman and the latter had soon overpowered the girl, torn the cloak from her shoulders and part of her dress.

Jeanette gave a cry of consternation and pitifully tried to put her dress in order. Panting heavily, Charlotte Penfield stepped back and surveyed her handiwork with a satisfied smile upon her lips. Adam Penfield, in the meantime, watched the affair with delighted interest.

'Now will you sign?' he asked silkily.

Jeanette shook her head frantically to and fro. 'No, no!' she cried tremulously. 'No, I will never sign it. They were my mother's, not yours; you have no right to them!'

The Squire's eyes blazed with rage and a frenzy seized hold of him. He was about to advance upon the girl when there came a sudden interruption. The door burst open and Jack Gregory, the Squire's head warden, appeared upon the threshold. He was swaying unsteadily from side to side and in his eyes there was a wild, glassy stare.

'I wanna see you, Squire,' he cried.

14

Jack Gregory was a small, wiry individual with a pinched face and narrow eyes. He had been employed by the Squire of Wake Manor for many years. His official position in the household was head warden, but he was also Penfield's right-hand man and thus knew a considerable amount about the Squire's affairs. Gregory liked the confidential position he held, for he knew it was to his personal advantage. Of late, however, the Squire had become unusually dictatorial, so Gregory considered, and he knew it was because Penfield's life's ambition was nearing fulfilment. As a consequence Gregory realised that his position was becoming somewhat dangerous.

On top of all this the warden considered he was not being paid sufficiently for his valuable services. The result had been, some weeks back, a heated argument with his master, and it was some time afterwards that Gregory had hit upon a little scheme of his own. Quite simply the scheme was blackmail.

And so it was that one evening, brooding on things in general, he had repaired to Jack's Retreat and, over a large punchbowl and rummer, speculated upon the vision of pursuing the dangerous game upon which he had decided. After a few drinks he thought it an excellent idea; after a few more he felt confident as to its successful outcome; following further drinks the fear that he normally felt for the Squire of Wake had miraculously disappeared. When he arose somewhat unsteadily from the table a little later he was filled with great courage and a bold determination to carry out his plan come what may. The Squire, he avowed to himself out loud, was a treacherous curmudgeon.

He mounted his horse and galloped back through the rain to the manor. Upon arrival he left his steed outside the front door and scrambled resolutely up the steps. In the short passage that opened out into the hall he stopped and listened. Voices came from the room on his left. For a second he hesitated, then, squaring his shoulders, he strode forward, opened the door and entered. He halted on the threshold and his eyes moved slowly round the room. Then he saw Adam Penfield standing, half turned, near the settee by the window.

'I wanna see you, Squire,' he cried.

Penfield swung round and glared furiously at the little man. 'Fool!' he roared. 'Get out!'

Gregory, however, took little heed. Instead he crooked one skinny finger and beckoned to the Squire. Muttering a curse, Adam Penfield hurried across to him. This gave the warden even greater confidence and he smiled broadly in a very superior manner.

'Get out, man,' breathed the Squire between his teeth.

Gregory looked hurt, then suddenly he glared back at his master with equal ferocity and said in a somewhat inebriated voice: 'I want twenty — I want twenty pounds from you, Penfield!'

The Squire stared at him in amazement, then slowly his expression changed and he gazed upon his head warden with sorrow and pity. 'Get out, Gregory,' Penfield murmured evenly. 'Get out, or I promise it will go badly with you!'

Jack Gregory grinned, no whit abashed, and he leaned forward and leered into Adam Penfield's smooth face. 'Give me twenty pounds, Penfield, or I shall have to tell our dear friend Constable Pucky a very pretty story.'

The Squire regarded his drunken and rebellious lieutenant contemptuously for some time, and before his master's penetrating eyes Gregory at last began to grow a little uneasy. Suddenly Penfield leaped back across the room to a desk standing against the far wall. Realising with dismay what his master's intention was, the head warden jumped hastily back into the passage, but the Squire had already grasped a loaded pistol and, cocking it, he swung round and fired straight at Gregory's chest. The warden gave a cry of pain and fell back against the wall of the passage. He coughed and then, with a great effort, began stumbling towards the front door, clutching his chest from whence blood welled profusely.

Penfield had already laid his hand upon a second pistol, ready loaded, and, watched wide-eyed by the two women, he raced out into the passage. Gregory was slowly and laboriously dragging himself up on to his horse, the driving rain making his task the harder. Penfield fired again but this time the shot went low and entered the warden's thigh. Still Gregory continued to pull himself up and at last he collapsed into the saddle and fell weakly forward across the horse's neck. He dug in his spurs with his last remaining ounce of strength. The horse leaped forward nervously and, with the warden holding the reins with one hand, raced away down the drive.

Cursing loudly, the Squire spun about and ran back into the hall. 'Bullard!' he roared. 'Bullard!'

This worthy came running affrightedly from the rear of the house. 'What is it, sir? What is it?'

'Ride after Gregory,' Adam Penfield cried. 'He is making for the village I think. Bring him back!'

'Yes, sir, yes, sir,' gasped Bullard, and the burly fellow ran hastily away to the stables.

'Senton!' roared Adam Penfield again.

The footman appeared immediately. 'Sir?'

'Tell Haggett and Lowy to go to the cellar.'

'Yes, sir.'

The Squire returned to the room at the front of the house and strode quickly over to Jeanette.

'Well, my dear girl, are you going to sign or are you not?'

Jeanette, who had been horrified by the way in which the Squire had handled his head warden, now gritted her teeth and shook her head, keeping her eyes lowered, frightened that he might strike her face again. Penfield pursed his lips, glanced at his wife and shrugged his shoulders. He bent down, grasped the girl's arm, pulled her to her feet and dragged her from the room.

They crossed the hall, Charlotte Penfield leisurely bringing up the rear, and entered the little room on the far side where the Squire had first spoken to Rob Welton. Penfield led the girl across to the other side and opened a small door in the corner. Jeanette, looking up, saw ahead a narrow stone passage dimly lit by flickering candles. Terror struck at her heart and she began struggling wildly, but it was quite useless; she could not escape the vice-like grip upon her arm, and she was dragged forward into the passage.

At the far end they turned a corner and came upon a number of stone steps leading down to an iron door at the bottom. Penfield descended, pulling the girl along behind him. She lost her footing once and nearly tumbled head-long, but the grip upon her arm steadied her and she reached the bottom safely. The Squire opened a door and entered the room beyond with Jeanette close behind. The sight that met the girl's eyes sent a cold shiver running down her spine.

The place had obviously once been a wine cellar but now, instead of barrels and cases, a number of strange-looking appliances lay about and Jeanette needed no telling that they were instruments of torture. Two men sat at a table in the middle of the room and when Penfield entered they rose to their feet and stood motionless awaiting his command. One was a tall, heavily built man, the other short and squat.

The Squire dragged the girl across to the far wall and, with the assistance of Lowy, the squat man, each wrist was locked in an iron ring embedded in the wall. Crazy with fear, Jeanette wanted to scream and scream again but she knew it would be of no use, and she stared at the blank, grey wall a few inches from her nose, her heart pounding so heavily she thought it would burst.

Charlotte Penfield sat down at the table, upon which stood a lantern, propped her head on her hand and watched interestedly, her eyes large and bright. The Squire grasped the top of the girl's dress and ripped it down so that her back was bared to the waist.

'Now, my girl,' hissed the Squire in her ear, 'you no doubt have guessed what we intend to do unless you sign that paper.'

Jeanette wanted to burst into tears and cry her heart out, but instead she slowly shook her head. 'No, no — I will not,' she whispered. 'You know it's not yours.'

Adam Penfield clenched his fists and then turned and nodded to Lowy. The man unhooked a heavy whip from a nail in the wall, strode across to the girl and, raising it high above his head, brought it down with a vicious swing across her back.

15

In the little room at the back of the Black Horse Inn sat the three highwaymen. Dick Palmer and Rob Welton were reclining in their chairs listening with awe to Will Snell, who was speaking at some length on the opposite sex. Prior to this Will had given a lecture on the art of smuggling.

Owing to the presence of Rob Welton the subject for which Dick and Will had specially visited the inn to discuss had as yet not been mentioned, and now Dick Palmer was beginning to wonder whether it ever would be — that evening at any rate. However, perhaps this was all to the good, because Palmer did not consider his garrulous friend was in any condition at the moment to discuss the matter — Wild Will was far from sober. The giant was sprawled in an ungainly manner in his chair staring up at the ceiling and waving his arms about in a dramatic way as he talked. At intervals he would stop to slake his apparently infinite thirst. Then, this ceremony completed, he would start off again with revivified energy and exuberance. Soon after, however, his speech would fade away to a mere drone and jumble of words, at which time he would reach forward for another drink.

As was to be expected, the ale eventually lost its power of stimulation and soon his listeners were unable to distinguish his words at all, and Wild Will began to dribble at the mouth like an overgrown baby and to gently slip forward in his seat until his wiry red beard dipped, in an undignified manner, in the spilt ale on the table.

Will had pointed out earlier that evening that it was not often anyone had the chance of drinking limitless quantities of free ale and, he had avowed, he intended taking full advantage of the situation. His friends had noted that he had carried out this intention to the best of his ability; they were now gazing upon the results.

Suddenly his mumblings ceased. He sat

up abruptly for a second and stared at them blankly, then he slumped forward over the table and in a minute was snoring lustily. Palmer feeling now somewhat jolly himself, was about to reach for his tankard when there came the sound of hurrying footsteps in the passage outside. The two men sat very still, glanced at each other questioningly and then grimly at the door. Palmer jumped quickly to his feet, ran round the table and shook Will Snell roughly by the shoulder, but there was no response from the giant — he was deep in slumber. He had chosen a most propitious moment, Dick thought, to go to sleep.

The two men stared at the door again, not sure what to do. Then as Palmer, calling to Welton, leaped towards the window, the door burst open and Timothy Pucky, the Chief Constable of Loughton, strode in, pistol in hand, his red face flushed and triumphant.

'Hold, Dick Palmer,' he cried.

The young highwayman faced about and glared at Pucky with frustrated fury.

'I arrest you,' announced the constable,

'for the murder of Simon Beckley.'

Standing behind Timothy Pucky was Robert Mason, the Keeper of Epping Forest, and behind him Hatchley, his assistant. All three officers held their pistols ready in their hands, their fingers crooked around the triggers, and there was no doubt they would fire if the occasion demanded.

Dick Palmer cursed beneath his breath, for he saw that he was cornered. 'You fool,' he growled. 'It was not me. Don't you know what goes on in this village?'

The Chief Constable did not answer but stared thoughtfully at the highway-man. It was obvious, however, that he did not understand what Palmer meant. 'I do and I know my job,' he cried stoutly. 'Who are these men with you?'

'Friends — they know nothing.'

'Ha — may be,' grunted Pucky. He looked at Welton. 'You come along too.'

The Constable then stepped quickly forward to the side of the highwaymen. 'Out you go to the bar room,' he ordered. 'I like not these cramped quarters.'

There was no escape, and with grim

faces Palmer and Welton walked slowly out of the room, followed closely down the passage by Mason and Hatchley. The Constable remained behind to poke his pistol in Will Snell's ribs, but he saw that the big fellow was not likely to give any trouble for some time to come. He left Will sprawled over the table and followed his men along the passage to the bar room at the front of the inn.

Already there were six or seven villagers gathered around the two highwaymen. Little Nicholas Wilken was there, his big brown eyes filled with consternation. Harry Murray had come out from behind the bar and was rubbing his hands and frowning in a most agitated manner.

'Now then, let's have some space,' cried the Constable. He turned to Palmer: 'Are those horses outside yours?' he asked.

Dick nodded: 'They are.'

'Fine. Have you anything to say before I lock you up in Loughton jail?'

'Nothing — except that I am innocent.'

The Chief Constable frowned slightly and gazed in a perplexed fashion at the young highwayman. He admitted to himself the lad looked little like a murderer. Ah, well, one could never tell. A silence had descended upon the company whilst these thoughts passed through Pucky's mind, broken only by the sound of the rain falling gently outside — the storm had abated. The villagers watched everything with delighted interest. Dick Palmer's brain was working overtime trying to think of some way out of the situation. It was a tight corner in which they had got themselves; some way of escape must be found. Palmer could not allow himself to be taken now or else all would be lost. But with so many present what hope had they?

Glancing sideways at Welton, Dick saw that the tall highwayman seemed little disturbed. He stood in a carefree, easy attitude with quite a cheerful expression on his face. What was the matter with the man — did he not wish to escape? Mason stood close to Dick Palmer, his pistol not an inch from the highwayman's chest, and upon the other side was Hatchley poised like a young tiger over Welton.

Pucky was about to speak when there was a sudden disturbance at the back of the room. Emily Murray appeared, her grey hair awry, a wild look in her eyes. She burst through the ring of villagers and came panting to the side of her husband.

'Harry!' she cried out in a fearful tone. The landlord swung about at her great tone of anxiety and grasped her roughly by the shoulder. All eyes turned upon Emily Murray.

'It's Jeanette,' she choked. 'She's — she's disappeared.'

A queer high-pitched groan escaped the lips of Harry Murray and immediately there was a buzz of voices; for all knew the lovely daughter of the landlord of the Black Horse Inn. Dick Palmer's face turned pale. The Chief Constable stepped forward.

'Watch these men,' he told Mason, and then he spoke quietly to Emily Murray. 'Tell me, what exactly happened?'

'I — I thought she was in the kitchen, but she's not. I've searched everywhere and called her; she's not here — she's gone!' Emily turned helplessly to her husband.

Dick Palmer tried to take a step forward and speak to Murray but Mason jabbed his pistol deep into his ribs and he dare not make a move. An icy cold feeling flowed through his veins and he stared blankly before him, momentarily stunned.

Suddenly above the hubbub of voices that now filled the room and the patter of the rain upon the window panes there came the familiar loud clatter of a horse's hooves upon the road across the green. The sound reached all ears in the bar room and for some reason there seemed something ominous and foreboding about it, and all at once a hushed silence fell upon the company. The horse drew nearer and the villagers glanced at one another nervously.

The Constable turned and gazed out of the window into the black night but he could see nothing. 'I wonder who this can be?' he murmured to himself.

The horse came to a halt by the corner of the inn, still out of sight, and there followed a strange quietness — not a sound except for the monotonous patter of the rain; the rider seemed to prefer to sit outside on his steed in the darkness, All at once a slithering noise reached the small crowd in the bar room and then a soft thud.

Turning to make sure Palmer and Welton were still well cared for, Timothy Pucky, with an impatient grunt, strode towards the door. But before he had got half way the sound of slow, dragging footsteps reached his ears. He halted. 'This is very strange,' he muttered.

The constable was about to continue when the the footsteps suddenly quickened and entered the door of the inn, and then a horrified gasp went up from the quaking villagers as a bedraggled man covered in blood appeared in the doorway of the bar room.

'It's Jack Gregory!' cried Hatchley.

But the Squire's head warden was in a terrible state. He wore no coat nor hat and one side of his body was covered in a mass of blood which oozed from a gaping wound in his chest. His clothes were torn, his breeches on his left leg were in shreds, and the hair upon his calf was matted with blood and dirt from a second wound.

He stood swaying gently back and forth just inside the threshold, staring in a vacant manner at the crowd of villagers. Then, without any fuss, he toppled forward and collapsed in a heap upon the floor.

The Constable leaped forward, dropped to one knee, and turned the man over and propped his head on his arm. The villagers, and Mason and Hatchley with their captives, quickly gathered around the wounded man. The landlord knelt down upon the other side and assisted the Constable to carry the warden over to a chair near the window. At that moment Gregory's eyes flickered open again.

'Who has done this?' Pucky asked softly. 'Tell me, Gregory, and he shall be brought to book.'

The head warden's eyes moved slowly round the sea of faces above him and at last they came to rest on Dick Palmer. 'I have something to say,' he whispered feebly, gazing intently up at the young highwayman. 'Listen — '

Gregory gave a sudden cough and spat blood. The Constable bent closer and the villagers moved nearer. 'What — what is it you wish to say, Gregory?' Pucky asked.

The warden sat up slightly, staring straight at Dick Palmer, and said very slowly: 'I — did — kill — Simon — Beckley!'

A soft gasp rose from the villagers. Dick Palmer jerked forward, his eyes gleaming triumphantly. 'Speak on,' he cried, terrified that here Gregory might stop. 'Why — why did you do it?'

Jack Gregory coughed again — he was finding it hard to breathe. 'It was done by — by the Squire's orders,' he choked hoarsely. 'Beckley had — found — out — too much!'

Palmer bent over him eagerly, ignoring Mason's effort to hold him back. The Constable glanced up at Mason. 'Release him,' he said quietly. The Keeper let go the highwayman immediately and Rob Welton was also released. The latter stepped quickly forward, a strange, agitated expression on his thin face. He touched Palmer on the shoulder. 'Dick

— Dick,' he whispered urgently.

The young highwayman glanced back over his shoulder, frowning. 'What — what is the matter, man?' he asked. But before Welton could speak there was an abrupt cry from Harry Murray:

'He's dead!'

Everybody looked quickly down at Jack Gregory. The warden's eyes were glassy and still, his head had fallen to one side, and his arms hung loosely to the floor. The Constable felt his pulse and then put his ear to the man's chest. He listened a while and then shrugged his shoulders and stood up. 'Yes, he is dead,' he agreed.

Silence filled the room, every man looking down with horrified solemnity upon the body of Jack Gregory slumped on the chair like a sack of corn.

'Dick — for God's sake listen,' came the sudden cry, and all eyes turned in surprise towards Rob Welton, who was tugging at Palmer's sleeve.

'Whatever is the matter?' queried the highwayman, pulling his arm away from Welton's grasp.

'Listen,' exclaimed Welton. 'May God

forgive my dastardly act — the Squire has Jeanette Murray!'

At first the full meaning of the words did not sink into Palmer's brain and for a second he stared blankly at the tall highwayman. Then he stepped quickly forward and glared into Rob Welton's eyes. The landlord moved nearer and Emily Murray gazed at Welton with one hand held over her lips to prevent a cry. At last Dick Palmer spoke, grinding out the words: 'What did you say, Welton?'

'The Squire — the Squire has the girl.'

Suddenly Palmer grasped the lapels of Welton's coat and shook him fiercely. 'Say that again,' he roared in a terrible tone.

'She — she is at the manor. I thought you — you killed Simon — I am his brother!'

A deathly silence followed as everybody present digested his amazing words, and Dick Palmer stared at the tall highwayman uncomprehendingly. At last, however, Palmer began to understand and he knew that he was now wasting his time at the inn. Without another word he let go of the tall highwayman and turned and faced the Chief Constable. He was just about to speak when he changed his mind and glanced across questioningly at Harry and Emily Murray. They understood him for they both nodded.

Dick turned back to Pucky. 'I think you should know, Constable,' he said in a quiet voice, 'that Jeanette Murray is really the daughter of Adam Penfield, the Squire of Wake Manor.'

Pucky stared back in amazement at the young highwayman and gave an astounded gasp. 'What foolish talk is this?' he cried.

'It is no foolish talk, Constable, but true,' replied Palmer. 'Here is her birth certificate,' and thereupon Dick produced the paper from his waistcoat pocket. The Constable took it and began reading. When he had finished he looked up questioningly at the highwayman, a perplexed frown upon his forehead.

'There is not time to explain the matter,' said Palmer grimly, taking the document back. 'The vital point is — the girl is in very great danger this very moment.' With that Dick Palmer turned and made his way quickly towards the door. For a few moments no one stirred behind him.

'Wait!' called Timothy Pucky suddenly. 'I will come too.' He swung about and beckoned to Mason and Hatchley and the three of them hurried after the highwayman. Rob Welton hesitated for a second and then he, too, followed Palmer. The latter was already at the side of Red Ruby when the four men joined him. He glanced at them but said no word, and they mounted their horses in silence. Within a minute, Dick Palmer in the lead, they were galloping out across the village green at a furious pace.

High Beach was left behind and they entered the forest, bent over their steeds and thundered through the black night, intent upon reaching Wake Manor with all possible speed. There was some shelter from the rain along the road as it wound through the forest but ahead was darkness, the trunks of the trees at the side of the highway seeming like black pillars.

Dick Palmer rode on recklessly, guiding

Red Ruby by his senses and by what he could remember of the road. Pucky, Mason, Hatchley and Welton kept as close behind him as they could, relying upon the highwayman to find his way.

Without warning Dick slowed down and the four behind nearly crashed into him. They had reached the fork. Palmer led the way into the Epping Road and soon they were at full tilt again. Gradually Dick pulled away from his four companions, for their steeds were no match for Red Ruby.

The highwayman had had little time to think over the amazing events of the past few hours. What filled his mind now was that Squire Penfield had taken Jeanette and he must, therefore, reach Wake Manor with all possible speed. This fact filled Palmer's brain to the exclusion of all else and and he raced along the road at a tremendous pace, the like of which the Constable, as he continued afterwards, had never seen equalled before — except perhaps by Dick Turpin!

Palmer seemed to be a part of his steed, and Red Ruby's slim, powerful legs flashed over the ground so swiftly that they were all but invisible, and the two flew through the night like some strange denizen of the forest.

The highwayman saw the gates of Wake Manor when only a few feet away and, swaying right over in the saddle, he took the corner into the drive at breathtaking speed and Red Ruby all but crashed into the trees on the far side. Dick's leg scraped against the bark of one tree, then they were past and on up the drive. In a minute the highwayman had leaped from his saddle and was standing looking up at the great doorway flanked by the giant pilasters. The doors were wide open. Palmer raced up the steps and strode quickly down the passage. He tried the door on his left and pushed it open. He stepped inside, pistol in his hand, but the room was empty.

The highwayman went out into the passage again and made his way along to the hall. He halted on the threshold and listened. A sombre silence lay over the manor and it seemed that the house was empty, for there was not a sign of life anywhere. At this moment Constable Pucky and the other three arrived. Palmer returned to the front of the house and met them as they came up the steps.

'The place seems empty,' he declared.

16

Dick Palmer led the way into the spacious hall and the five men looked swiftly about them, on the alert for any attack. But not a sound of any description was to be heard — the manor appeared to be deserted.

'We shall have to search the place,' Pucky observed.

'Then we must take care,' said Dick Palmer. 'There may yet be a chance of surprising the Squire — if he is still here.'

'Let us search these rooms leading off from the hall,' suggested the Constable, 'then assemble here again before going further.'

The men nodded and they broke up and began the search, each one covering a section of the hall. It was Rob Welton who entered the small study at the back. On his previous visit he had not noticed the door at the rear of the room which led to the cellar and now, seeing that it was empty, he withdrew, with no further examination. The five men completed their search without result and they gathered in the centre of the hall again.

'A long passage over there leads to the servant's quarters,' said Mason. 'I had not time to search it — shall I now?'

'No — wait,' replied the Constable, 'we must not be rash.'

'That's true,' agreed Palmer. 'I think we had better keep together.'

At that moment footsteps were heard coming from the rear of the house. The door leading to the servant's quarters opened and the five men beheld an old, white-haired man enter the hall. Rob Welton reached for his pistol.

'Hold,' cried Dick Palmer, 'it's Benjamin Tapner.'

'And who might he be?' asked the Constable.

'He's the Squire's groomsman, but an honest fellow — he should prove of help to us.'

Benjamin Tapner ambled across the hall towards them, a large grin wrinkling his aged face. 'Evenin' to 'ee, gennelmen,' he greeted cheerfully. He did not appear at all surprised to find five strangers in his master's house.

'Evening to you, Benjamin,' replied Dick Palmer. 'Tell me, my good fellow — where is the Squire?'

Tapner glanced quickly about him, apparently thinking the Squire might be hiding in a corner of the bare hall. 'Haven't you seen him at all?' he asked.

'No.'

'Ah,' grunted the groomsman and he glanced up at Dick Palmer with a strange expression in his eyes. 'I suggest yon try the cellar, my boy,' he said quietly.

Palmer was quick to note the old man's solemn tone, and he asked grimly: 'Where is the cellar?'

'See yonder door?'

'Yes.'

'At the back of that room you will find another door — a small one. Behind it is a passage leading to the cellar.'

'Thank you, Benjamin,' Dick grunted, and he led the way cross the hall to the room the groomsman had indicated. He opened the door and stepped boldly inside. Now that it had been pointed out the small door was quite easy to see. It was half open.

'Ha!' Palmer breathed, and when the others had joined him, he stepped over and pulled the door wide open. The passage beyond was empty, except for four flickering candles that threw shadowy, yellow lights upon the walls. In single file the men crept stealthily forward, moving as softly as they could upon the bare stones. Dick soon reached the corner of the passage where the steps led down to the cellar door, and here he halted. Constable Pucky closed up behind him.

'Can you hear anything?' he whispered.

Palmer shook his head. The quietness about them was cold and hostile and the five men could not help but feel a little uneasy. Taking a deep breath Palmer began to descend the steps, and the others followed him carefully. Abruptly the silence was broken by a scraping sound as Hatchley caught the side of his boot against the wall. The five men stopped dead, their hearts beating wildly.

The quietness that followed seemed more intense than ever.

Palmer reached the bottom and waited until the others had gathered behind him. He conversed in a low tone with the Chief Constable for a short time as to their best plan of action. At last they decided what to do and Palmer reached forward and tried the handle of the door. It turned noislessly and the door opened. Glancing back to make sure his four companions were ready, Dick then flung it open and leaped forward into the cellar, the Constable, Mason, Hatchley and Welton close behind, their pistols drawn.

Immediately Dick Palmer realised that they had fallen into a trap.

'Down your weapons and turn around!' came a cry.

The voice came from directly behind them by the door. Reluctantly they dropped their pistols on the stone floor, the loud clatter echoing and re-echoing around the cellar. Dick Palmer cursed bitterly, realising now the foolhardiness of their move. Slowly they faced about and beheld the Squire, with three of his men, lined up against the wall behind the door, pistols in hand. One of them was Bullard, the fellow Penfield had sent after Jack Gregory. Then Palmer saw Jeanette — huddled in a corner with Charlotte Penfield standing guard over her. Charlotte had just taken her hand away from the girl's mouth, for Jeanette had tried to scream a warning to Palmer. Impulsively the highwayman stepped forward towards her.

'I should not, if I were you,' cried the Squire warningly, a sardonic smile upon his face. Palmer halted, glared at Penfield, and reluctantly stepped back again. He realised that he would be of no use to Jeanette dead. The Squire and his men began moving forward deliberately, their pistols levelled.

'This will not help you, Penfield,' said Pucky quietly.

'No?' grinned the Squire. 'We shall see.' He glanced curiously at Rob Welton. 'And to what do I owe this pleasant visit?' he asked.

Welton was silent for a moment and then he said grimly, 'I made a foolish mistake.'

Adam Penfield shrugged his shoulders, not understanding, and obviously not particularly interested. He forced his captives back into a corner of the cellar and left Bullard, Lowy and Haggett to stand guard. He then walked over to Jeanette and, grasping her slim arm, dragged her across to the wall again. The girl struggled furiously, taking new heart at the presence of her lover, but it was of no avail, and for the second time her wrists were clamped in the iron rings.

Dick Palmer watched these proceedings with blazing eyes and Timothy Pucky, seeing that the young highwayman was about to spring forward to her defence, laid a restraining hand upon his arm. 'Wait a little longer, my friend,' he whispered.

Palmer now noticed the terrible marks of the whip on Jeanette's back and, not hearing the Constable's words, he took a step forward, his lips set grimly. Bullard levelled his pistol threateningly. Palmer looked at him contemptuously and hesitated, but he realised it was of no use trying to get by — he would be just shot down. He would have to wait for a more opportune moment. Clenching his fists, he stepped back again.

'Fire, if he moves another inch,' called the Squire. He then stepped over to the table and picked up the whip.

'If it be her birth certificate you require,' cried Palmer, 'I have it.' He dived into his waistcoat pocket and produced the paper and threw it over to the Squire.

'Dick — don't, don't,' called out Jeanette.

Adam Penfield smiled, seeming highly amused, and picked up the paper thoughtfully from the floor. 'Thank you, but I'm awfully sorry, it's of no importance now,' he said softly. 'However, it will make matters a little easier.'

There was a distracted look on Dick Palmer's face and his hand was shaking as he raised it to wipe the sweat from his brow. His eyes swept around the room, trying to think of some way of turning the tables. But it seemed there was none.

'You, I take it,' said Constable Pucky suddenly, as the Squire raised the whip, 'killed Jack Gregory.'

Adam Penfield lowered the whip. 'That is quite correct,' he replied cheerfully. 'He, too, became dangerous.'

'Then you did order the killing of Simon Beckley?' snapped Pucky.

The Squire looked hurt. 'But of course, my dear fellow — he interfered, the fool.'

Dick Palmer watched the three men that guarded them carefully whilst the Squire and the Constable conversed, but they held their pistols in a resolute fashion and were obviously not afraid to use them. The highwayman saw that fear of their master made them grimly determined to carry out their job efficiently.

Charlotte Penfield had sat down by the table again and now was listening to and watching with great intentness the dramatic play that was being enacted before her eyes.

'What is your reason — what is the purpose of these wicked deeds?' cried Pucky, losing some of his initial calmness.

Adam Penfield smoothed his black wig with one slim hand. He was delighted with himself and the whole affair, but he still retained a cautious air. He strolled over to the table and leaned languidly against the edge. He flicked the whip lazily through the air.

'I will tell you,' he said considerately, bending down to give his wife a kiss upon her powdered forehead. 'My first partner in life — you no doubt have heard of her — was of French nationality.'

Jeanette turned round at these words, as far as the rings would allow, and stared intently at the Squire of Wake Manor.

Dick Palmer relaxed. The Constable's ruse to distract temporarily the Squire's attention from Jeanette had worked.

Greatly pleased with the fact that he was the centre of attraction, Penfield continued his story with enthusiasm. 'She came from an old French family,' — there was a contemptuous note in his voice — 'and it was their foolish practice to hand their valuable heirlooms and jewels down through the family. The fortune had been settled upon my first wife for life and for some ridiculous reason,' — the Squire now spoke heatedly — 'upon her death they passed to her daughter absolutely. When I married Louisa I unfortunately did not know this fact.' The Squire frowned and suddenly swished the whip angrily through the air. He felt in his coat pocket and produced an ornamental snuff box and he took a pinch and filled each nostril. He replaced the box and continued the story.

'She gave birth to a baby girl before — she died,' he remarked, staring thoughtfully at the tip of his whip.

Silence followed and one or two swift looks were cast in the direction of Jeanette. The Squire nodded reflectively. 'Yes,' he said, 'she is my daughter.'

The silence was broken by Jeanette herself. 'What did my mother die of?' she whispered.

'Well,' replied Adam Penfield deliberately. 'I placed her in a room in the north wing and, I am afraid — I forgot all about her!' The Squire stared across at Jeanette with a strange blank expression.

A long, horrified gasp escaped the girl's lips and abruptly she fell limply against the wall. A grim stillness had settled down in the cellar. Charlotte Penfield sat unconcernedly at the table, fanning herself. The Squire smiled, amused at the effect his words had had upon his listeners.

'The baby was in the way,' he went on, ' — I left her in the forest. Unfortunately — most unfortunately, she was picked up by the damned Murrays. This I didn't discover until some time later.'

Adam Penfield warmed to his subject, and everybody watched and listened with fascination. Bullard and the other two guards stood firm, their pistols steady. At that moment Dick Palmer recollected that he had seen a large wooden club when first he entered the cellar, hanging upon the wall behind him. Watching his guards carefully he slowly backed up close to the wall. Stealthily he raised his arm and moved his fingers along towards it.

'To cut a long story short,' declared the Squire, 'having seen the trustees of the Martilliére jewels and discovering that the girl was alive, it became necessary that I find her birth certificate.' Penfield flicked the whip through the air again and then continued: 'With this and her death certificate the trustees agreed to hand the fortune to me.'

He stopped and smiled cheerfully around at his audience. 'Enjoying the little tale?' he asked.

'Yes,' snapped Constable Pucky, his red face redder than ever. 'Already you have told me enough to hang you many, many times!'

The smile vanished from the Squire's face. 'It will be many more times than that Constable,' he sneered, ' — when I have finished with you and your foolish friends.'

The Chief Constable took a deep breath and stared in astonishment at Adam Penfield. 'You dare not,' he gasped.

The Squire stared back contemptuously and then abruptly he burst into a high gurgle of laughter. He turned to his wife to see what she thought of the joke. Charlotte smiled slightly but made no remark. Timothy Pucky had received his reply and he relapsed into grim silence.

Penfield's unpleasant laughter subsided and there was left a cynical sneer upon his lips. 'Where was I?' he asked.

'I know where you will be,' grunted young Hatchley.

The Squire frowned, but he ignored the remark. 'Ah, yes,' he said. 'Well, eventually — after a long time — I found out from Sally Burke, who was once Louisa's handmaiden, that my wife had spoken of a ring when she was dying.'

At the mention of Sally Burke's name Dick Palmer suddenly remembered the day when first he came to High Beach. He remembered he had stopped at the little cottage on the edge of the village and joined a small crowd of people at the door. The Squire had ridden up and entered the cottage and the woman had spoken secretly to him. Yes, Palmer recalled the incident clearly now — so that is what the old handmaiden had whispered in the Squire's ear!

Whilst these thoughts were passing through Palmer's mind, his fingers continued to steal along the wall towards the club. His arm was nearly outstretched now, but still he could only feel the cold, damp wall. His efforts remained unnoticed, however, for the light from the lamp upon the table was not strong enough to illuminate the corners of the cellar.

'I followed this up,' went on the Squire, now thoroughly enjoying himself. 'I discovered that a special ring had been made for Louisa by a London jeweller. Then I realised what she had done. You — ' the Squire jerked his head towards Jeanette, ' — held your birth certificate all the time, but you never knew it. The document, as you know, was in the hollow mounting of the ring you wore.'

Adam Penfield flicked the whip towards Jeanette's back in a playful manner, and it licked across her bare skin and momentarily an inflamed line appeared. Jeanette gave a slight gasp and the iron rings rattled on her wrists as she sagged weakly against the wall.

Dick Palmer's face paled and he clenched his fists with rage, but he was helpless, he could not go to her assistance.

'I tried many ways to obtain that piece of paper,' the Squire snapped, 'but all proved unsuccessful.' Abruptly his demeanour changed and he glared angrily across the cellar at Palmer.

'You, you young hound,' he cried between his teeth, ' — you made things awkward. You forced me to my present move — taking the girl herself. If you had kept your meddlesome nose out of my affairs, none of you would be here now.'

The Squire angrily flicked the whip through the air again. 'But it's simpler,' he grunted. 'She will sign a document now handing over the entire fortune.'

All at once Penfield had changed again and was smiling benignly upon his audience. 'That is what I intend to make her do,' he said sweetly. 'She will sign it — eventually — I assure you.'

The Squire stepped forward then and spoke to Jeanette. 'Well, my dear, are you going to sign?'

Dick Palmer felt feverishly along the wall. He was partly hidden from view now behind Mason, but the club was still out of reach. He stared anxiously at Jeanette. 'Sign it — sign it, Jeanette,' he called, 'it's not all the world!'

'No — no, I cannot, Dick,' she replied

desperately. 'The jewels are mine — I will not let him possess them — for my mother's sake!'

The Squire swore profusely, his eyes blazed with rage and suddenly he raised the whip high over his head and brought it down with all his strength on Jeanette's back. A terrible scream of pain rang out and echoed and re-echoed around the cellar.

The blood drained away from Dick Palmer's face and his eyes stood out — huge and staring — and a nauseating feeling took hold of him so that he felt dizzy. The Squire's three henchmen remained steady, their faces expressionless. Palmer gazed at them frantically, trying to see any sign of compassion in their features, but there was none and he knew it would be foolhardy to go to Jeanette's help. He would never reach her alive.

An unpleasant, almost devilish, smile hovered around the Squire's lips and there was a wild gleam in his eyes as he raised the whip again.

'Please sign it, Jeanette,' Dick Palmer

called, his voice full of anguish.

Jeanette saw the great shadow of Penfield's raised arm upon the wall above her and she gave a moan. 'I will sign — I will sign,' she whispered, in so low a tone that some did not hear her, then her head fell forward upon her chest.

Palmer gave an audible sigh of relief and the tense atmosphere relaxed. With a delighted grin Penfield stepped forward and released Jeanette from the iron rings. He put his hands beneath her arms, for she seemed incapable of standing, and helped her across to the chair by the table that Charlotte Penfield had that moment vacated. The couple were now quite considerate as to Jeanette's comfort; there were triumphant smiles upon their faces.

Writing materials were all ready upon the table and a quill was placed in Jeanette's hand. The Squire produced the document and set it down before her and pointed to the place where he wished her to sign. Slowly and wearily Jeanette scratched out her name and a hush settled over everybody as she did so. Charlotte Penfield leaned over, her pale, blue eyes shining brightly. So close was she that Jeanette could feel her hot breath tickling the weals upon her back and could smell her heavy perfume. The woman snatched the paper up when Jeanette had finished and stared closely at it, wild triumph in her eyes. The Squire called to one of his henchmen.

'Bullard — you have seen who this girl is. Come here and make your mark upon this paper.'

The burly fellow pocketed his pistol and hurried over to the table. Very laboriously he signed his name, breathing heavily the while, as if it were some great physical exertion.

'Good!' exclaimed the Squire. 'Go back.'

Bullard obediently returned to his station, pulled out his pistol and levelled it at the five men in the corner again.

'Now you, Lowy,' called the Squire, 'you have seen her birth certificate.'

John Lowy, the squat man, came over to the table, signed his name and returned to his place, as Bullard had done. Penfield rubbed his hands with glee and gazed over his wife's shoulder at the document on the table. Charlotte picked it up, folded it, and carefully pushed it down beneath her tight bodice. The Squire grinned and nodded approvingly. He turned and stared sadly at the five men in the corner. He glanced at Jeanette, who had now fallen forward across the table, the light from the lamp gleaming on the red weals that stretched across her back. Penfield touched the marks curiously with one slim, manicured finger, but the girl did not stir — she had fainted.

The Squire looked up at the men in the corner again. 'Now, my dear friends, seeing that you know so much,' he said slowly, 'I am afraid I must kill you all!'

Young Hatchley gave a slight gasp, but the others remained silent, their lips tightening grimly. No one spoke. The Squire looked slightly annoyed.

'You, Palmer,' he said. 'I think I will keep you to the last. In fact,' he added, raising his voice, 'you can watch your sweet Jeanette die first.'

Dick Palmer, however, was not listening, for just at that moment his fingers had touched the cold handle of the club on the wall behind him. The Constable was watching anxiously out of the corner of his eye. Robert Mason surreptitiously moved a little further to one side, for he guessed the young highwayman's intention. His burly frame now partly obscured Palmer from the sight of the three henchmen.

But at that moment Dick Palmer paused in his reach for the club for, with amazement, he saw that the iron door behind the Squire's back was slowly opening. Somebody was coming into the cellar!

17

At the Black Horse Inn the bar room was crowded and there was a great hubbub of excited voices, for the news of the recent incidents at the inn had spread quickly through High Beach. Some villagers, delighted that the Squire was in trouble, openly displayed their approval; others, however, feared to portray their feelings and they sat at their tables listening, with lugubrious expressions, to their more garrulous friends. A few spoke darkly of impending calamity — for was not the village cursed with such a Squire? But little notice was taken of these doleful fellows.

The story of Jack Gregory's last moments in the land of the living was told and re-told and the true details eventually became somewhat distorted. Jim Pegley, the blacksmith's assistant, had never been anywhere near the inn that day, nevertheless he told a most horrible tale, with great relish, to two large old women who sat at a table, their big glasses of gin untouched, listening to him with ears cocked and their eyes as big as apples.

Harry Murray, the landlord, stood behind the bar watching the noisy crowd in silence, taking no part in the wild discourse. Between orders he remained very still, his squat, heavy frame straight and taut, for he waited for sound of the return of Dick Palmer and Constable Pucky and his men. At the front door stood Emily, gazing out across the village green towards the gap in the line of cottages upon the far side where the Loughton Road re-entered the forest.

It was the words of Jeremy Higgins, the village cobbler, that reminded Harry Murray of the man in the room at the back of the inn.

'As I remembers,' said Higgins, to an interested audience, the whole thing started when these two gennelmen comes marchin' in 'ere and the landlord goes to meet — '

Harry Murray did not wait to hear any more, but swung around and hurried out of the bar. He ran down the corridor at the rear and entered the passage, stepped across to the door of the little room and swung it open. Will Snell was still there — sprawled over the table like a huge bear, mouth wide open, snoring lustily. It was surprising nobody had heard such stentorian noises.

The landlord walked back to the door and poked his head into the passage. 'Emily,' he yelled. In a minute his wife came hurrying down the passage, an anxious frown upon her soft face. Harry pointed at Will Snell. 'Watch him,' he told her, 'whilst I fetch a pail of water.' Emily nodded and went inside the room.

The landlord strode away, collected a large pail from the kitchen and, stepping out into the yard, filled it from the pump by the stable door He retraced his steps to the little room, the pail filled to the brim. He stepped up to the side of Will Snell raised the pail high in the air, and then tipped the contents in a long, sparkling stream over the giant's head. The result was quite startling.

Will gave a loud hoot and leaped some

distance from his seat, thrashing the air wildly with his mighty arms. He blinked his eyes and shook his head like a massive bull, stared down at the dripping table and then across at the landlord who still held the pail in his hand. He scratched his thick, red hair, rubbed his eyes and glared at Harry Murray.

'What's this?' he roared.

'I'll tell you,' replied the landlord quickly, 'but one moment,' and he turned to his wife. 'Tell Nicholas to come here immediately.' Emily nodded obediently and left the room.

'Listen,' exclaimed Harry. 'The Squire has taken Jeanette. The Constable, Dick and the others have ridden to the Manor.'

Wild Will blinked and shook his shaggy head. He gazed rather vacantly at the landlord, then slowly his brain began to clear.

'Jumping catfish,' he breathed. 'Then it's as Dick feared?'

'Yes — Jack Gregory, the Squire's head warden, is in the bar, dead — killed by the Squire,' Murray informed him. 'But he spoke before he died and admitted

— in front of the Chief Constable — to killing Beckley.'

'That is fine,' cried Will. 'All is not lost then.'

'You wanted me, sir?' It was the timid voice of Nicholas Wilken, the ostler, who had appeared at the door.

'Yes, Nicholas,' replied the landlord, swinging round. 'Where is this gentleman's horse?'

'I put him in the stable, sir — nicely quartered, he is.'

'Well, fetch him out, saddle him and bring him round to the front — haste away now.'

The ostler nodded quickly and disappeared. Harry Murray turned back to Will Snell. 'So Dick is cleared — all blame has been taken from him.'

'Ha — that is good news indeed.'

'Here is more. This friend of yours — the tall, thin one — is Simon Beckley's brother. He it was that arranged for the Squire to take Jeanette.'

'Beckley's brother?' cried Will amazed. 'Blood and thunder! I might have guessed it. But why — what was his reason?'

'He believed Dick killed his brother and sought revenge.'

'The dirty blackleg!'

'No — it's not so. He repents, for he has gone with Dick to the Manor.'

Will Snell gave a heavy grunt and strode towards the door. 'Avast,' he cried. 'Let me away — may I be stricken with the plague if matters don't go well with Dick for the want of a strong arm.'

Harry Murray hurried after him as he strode mightily down the passage to the front of the inn. The villagers flocked to the door of the bar at the sound of his great step and thunderous voice, but they soon retreated at sight of him, and Will Snell sailed by like a man-o'-war.

Nicholas was ready for the giant, holding, with no little trouble, the reins of the powerful black stallion. The steed was snorting and stamping in a right wild manner, for he knew his master was about to take the warpath. The villagers crowded to the door and watched with interest.

'What avails you?' cried the giant to the stallion.

The horse thereupon glanced quickly round at his master, gave a great snort and reared high into the air with a shrill whinny of excitement. Poor Nicholas was all but thrown to the ground, but he held on grimly.

'The villain knows what is afoot,' Will Snell grunted. He laid his hands upon the reins and immediately the stallion quieted. The ostler, who stood back now, saw, however, that the great horse was quivering and panting with excited anticipation, his muscles strained and taut — he would be off like a cannon directly the word was given.

Will turned to the landlord. 'Do not fret, Harry — the son of Dick Turpin won't return without Jeanette — make no mistake o' that.' The giant then vaulted into the saddle.

'Farewell,' he cried and, with a dramatic wave of his hand, he dug his spurs deep into the flanks of the black stallion. Almost simultaneously the horse gave a powerful jerk with his hind legs and then leaped forward into the night like a thunderbolt.

As they charged across the village green Wild Will gave out a loud cry and the sound echoed and re-echoed about the little cottages, disturbing many a family at the fireside. The highwayman kept up a fast pace and it did not take him long to reach Wake Manor. He entered the drive and slowed down, and when he saw the sombre, dark building before him, he dismounted and tethered his horse amongst the trees out of sight. He went forward again on foot.

Henry Senton, the Squire's footman, was a timid fellow and it was most unfortunate for him that, having hidden himself in the servants' quarters earlier that evening, knowing full well what went on in the cellar, he should have decided to sneak out and take a stroll on the lawn in front of the manor. So it was that Will Snell espied him as he paraded slowly up and down. The giant bore silently down upon the unsuspecting footman, a wicked gleam in his eye.

The first intimation Henry had that he was not alone was a light tap upon the shoulder. With a scream of terror he spun round and found himself staring into a huge, ferocious, red-bearded face. His mouth dropped wide open.

'Where's your master?' boomed Will Snell.

Henry nearly jumped out of his skin. So frightened was he that his reply came immediately. 'In the cellar — he's in the cellar — you'll find him in the cellar,' he blurted out, holding up one hand in front of his face, afraid the giant might strike him.

Will Snell knew at once that the footman was telling the truth, but he glared in a terrible manner at him to make quite sure. Henry quaked in every limb. 'It's the truth — it's the honest truth, sir,' he screamed. 'He's there with a number of folk.'

'Ah, is that so?' cried Will, his eyes gleaming. 'Most interesting. Come, show me the way.'

Henry Senton shrank away, gazing with horror into Will Snell's bloodshot eyes. 'No, no, that I dare not do, sir,' he whimpered. 'The Squire would kill me!'

Will frowned impatiently. He had no

time to bandy words with the fellow. 'Show me, then,' he cried, 'where this cellar is situated. When you have done that you may jump in yonder pond for all I care.'

'Yes, yes,' nodded the footman, 'I will do that,' and he led the way towards the house. They entered through a small door at the back, ascended a flight of stone steps, traversed a long carpeted passage and arrived in the hall. Senton walked over to the study, opened the door and halted a few feet inside. He pointed at the small door on the far side of the room. 'That is it,' he whispered. 'Through there, along the passage and down the steps.'

'Good!' grunted Will. 'Is there any other entrance?'

'No, this is the only one.'

'You better be telling the truth,' growled the giant.

'I am — I am!' cried the footman.

'Well, then, my fine fellow, return to your room and stir not, or it will go badly with you.'

Henry Senton nodded energetically, hardly believing he to be let off so lightly. He turned and scurried across the hall and disappeared through the door to the servants' quarters. When he had gone Will Snell indulged in a quiet chuckle and then, looking to his pistols to see that they were cocked, he stepped into the study. He crossed the room without a sound, the light from the candles in the hall shining through and lighting the way. Very carefully he opened the small door Senton had pointed out to him and gazed along the narrow passage beyond. It was deserted except for the flickering candles set in sconces along the wall. Will listened intently but not a sound disturbed the deep silence.

Leaving the door partly open he crept down the passage like a huge cat, his great shadow floating along the wall before him. He reached the top of the stairs and stood there poised, for the sound of men's voices now reached his ears. With uncanny quietness he glided down the steps, and upon reaching the bottom he again looked to his pistols. Satisfied that they were ready for discharge, he listened for a few moments to the voices that reached him from inside the cellar. From what he heard he realised that the Squire's attention was taken up with something in the cellar and that the fellow didn't expect to be disturbed. Will reached forward and grasped the handle firmly and then he began slowly opening the door.

18

Dick Palmer, upon seeing the cellar door slowly opening, glanced quickly at the Squire's three henchman, but none of them had noticed his surprised expression. In actual fact Haggett, Lowy and Bullard were finding it a full-time job trying to watch their five captives all at the same time. Dick tightened his grip upon the club behind him and watched the door closely. Whoever was entering the cellar at that moment was a friend, else why should he open the door in such a surreptitious manner?

Adam Penfield had produced a pistol and was in the act of cocking it. He smiled benignly at Dick Palmer, half hidden by Robert Mason, and then turned to the girl, who had fallen forward across the table, and very deliberately aimed the pistol at her bare back.

A deathly silence settled upon the room — a silence filled with horror, for few had believed the Squire would carry out such a cruel, cold-blooded action. Even Charlotte Penfield looked a little surprised and glanced wonderingly at her husband. But the Squire was not at all bothered, in fact the opposite was the case for his lips were parted in a delighted grin and there was a glitter in his eyes. And at that moment Dick Palmer almost cried out loud with joy, for a large red beard had appeared around the edge of the cellar door. But the blood drained away from his face when he saw that Adam Penfield's finger was tightening on the trigger.

'Will!' Palmer cried out in a shrill voice, 'Will! Stop the Squire!'

'Avast!' roared Wild Will in reply, stepping into the cellar and glancing aggressively about him. Momentarily the Squire's attention was distracted and that was Will Snell's chance. Quickly appreciating the situation, he took aim and discharged his pistol at Penfield. The bullet struck the Squire's arm and with a cry of pain he dropped his pistol and clutched the wounded limb.

Bullard, Lowy and Haggett spun

around at the sound of the shot and immediately Palmer went into action. He grasped the club firmly and swung it viciously over his head at John Lowy. The man did not have a chance. The blow smashed down upon the crown of his head and he toppled forward to the floor like a felled tree.

Rob Welton leaped at Haggett, but the big fellow saw him just in time and fired. The tall highwayman staggered, almost fell, swayed on his feet and then came on again and grappled with the burly henchman. Timothy Pucky was not long in following Welton's example and he soon was in grim combat with Bullard. Hatchley raced forward to the assistance of Welton and Robert Mason went to the help of the Constable. In the meantime Dick Palmer advanced upon the Squire his club raised menacingly.

Will Snell, slinging his useless pistol across the cellar, charged towards Penfield from the other side. The Squire glanced from one to the other, fear in his dark eyes, and he glanced anxiously about the room for some means of escape. He saw the little pile of pistols three or four feet away dropped by Palmer and his men when first they entered the cellar. He stepped swiftly across to them and grasped one in each hand and then turned and fired straight at Dick Palmer. The bullet entered the highwayman's right shoulder and halted him and the club slipped from his nerveless fingers. He stood holding his shoulder with one hand and swaying gently back and forth.

Swinging to the left, Adam Penfield aimed with his other pistol at Jeanette Murray, but before he could pull the trigger Will Snell was upon him, roaring like a lion, and in a minute they were locked in deadly combat. Penfield knew the tables were turning and he fought like a maniac and seemed suddenly to have gained the strength of two men. For a moment he was the equal of Will Snell, and they staggered back and forth across the cellar battling for the ascendancy.

Charlotte Penfield had scurried into a corner and there she crouched, watching the scene with terror in her eyes. She was very pale and the whiteness of her skin showed up beneath her rouge and powder. Dick Palmer walked unsteadily over to Jeanette and lifted her up from the table. The girl's eyes flickered open and she stared about her with wonder at the raging fight. She glanced up at Dick Palmer and saw the patch of blood on his shoulder.

'You are hurt!' she cried.

'I'm all right,' Dick grunted, leaning weakly against the table. 'Retrieve the document at all costs,' and he pointed across the room at Charlotte Penfield huddled in the corner.

Jeanette nodded and started across the room towards the woman. Charlotte, seeing the girl coming, gave a pitiful gasp and dashed towards the door. Jeanette was prepared, however, and gritting her teeth — for her back was painful — she jumped forward and barred the way. The two women glared hatefully at one another and then Jeanette reached forward and grasped Charlotte by the neck and shook her like a rat. The elder woman gave no resistance whatsoever and suddenly she began sobbing.

'Where is the paper?' Jeanette cried. 'Where is it?'

'She has it here,' called Palmer, pointing down at his chest.

Jeanette gave a delighted laugh and promptly tore Charlotte Penfield's bodice wide open, revealing the woman's heavy bosom encased in a tightly laced corset. Thereupon Charlotte began howling like a baby. Sticking out of the top of her corset was the document and Jeanette quickly grasped it and tore it into tiny pieces.

Haggett had knocked Welton to the floor and now John Hatchley was in a sore plight. Mason, seeing this, ran to his help, for Timothy Pucky had his own battle well in hand and was at that moment banging Bullard's thick skull against the wall. Bullard could not stand this, solid fellow though he was, and at last he slipped unconscious to the floor and lay in a crumpled heap.

The Constable ran to the centre of the cellar and picked up two of the remaining pistols. He then advanced upon Will Snell and Adam Penfield, who were still fighting like wild cats in a corner of the cellar. The Squire was growing weaker however — his great initial strength was disappearing. Will Snell now had a tremendous grip on his neck.

'Surrender, Penfield,' cried the Chief Constable in a commanding tone, 'or I fire!'

For answer the Squire turned and spat on the floor and then quite suddenly, he had slipped from Will Snell's grasp. He delved into his waistcoat and produced a small, wicked looking knife and with this he advanced in a crouching position upon the Chief Constable. Will Snell hesitated, debating whether to follow, but he decided against it.

'Take no more steps, Penfield,' warned Constable Pucky grimly, levelling his pistols. 'I am not afraid to kill you.'

Dick Palmer was leaning against the table with his arm around Jeanette. She had taken the opportunity whilst the men were engaged to adjust her dress, and now a little colour had returned to her cheeks. They watched the Squire in silence, for it was quite obvious what would happen if he failed to stop his advance on the Chief Constable.

Penfield, however, kept on, leaning forward, glaring out beneath his dark eyebrows in an almost fiendish manner at Timothy Pucky. His black wig was hanging off the side of his head and his lips were drawn back in a hideous snarl. He held the knife raised threateningly, and as he drew nearer to the Constable he gave a little chuckle, as if relishing what was to come.

Again Pucky called out to him: 'Don't be foolish Penfield. I cannot miss with both barrels. Stop before it's too late.'

The Squire grinned but made no reply. He raised the knife higher and continued to creep nearer. Suddenly he leapt forward like a tiger. 'Never will you get me, Pucky!' he screamed. 'Never will you — '

Abruptly his words were cut short by the explosion from the two pistols as the Chief Constable discharged them simultaneously. The Squire of Wake Manor appeared to halt in mid-air and hover there like an evil bird of prey, then he crashed to the floor not two paces distance from Timothy Pucky.

The silence that followed was short-lived, for almost immediately it was broken by a heavy slithering noise at the far end of the cellar. Mason and Hatchley had just overcome Haggett and that worthy slowly slid down the wall to the floor. Hatchley hurried over to Rob Welton, who still lay motionless where he had fallen. Dick Palmer, Jeanette, Pucky and Will Snell joined him, for the fight was over. Hatchley bent down and turned Welton on to his back. The highwayman's eyes were closed. Quickly the Constable dropped to one knee and felt Rob Welton's pulse. In a minute he rose again and shook his head grimly. 'I am afraid he is dead,' he exclaimed.

Jeanette gave a little gasp and turned away. Dick Palmer stared down for some time at the long body of the highwayman. 'He was a friend,' he murmured, 'a friend; he has proved that.'

Without warning Palmer staggered back and almost fell, but Will Snell was there and he caught his friend and steadied him. Jeanette hurried to Dick's side.

'You are weak from loss of blood,' cried she. The girl eased off his coat and his upper arm was revealed covered in blood.

'He needs a doctor,' Jeanette cried.

Timothy Pucky nodded. 'Yes, let us return to the hall. I think we have finished here. We will ask the old groomsman to harness a coach and horses; the Squire owned one I know.' He led the way across the cellar and they ascended the stairs, Palmer leaning on Will Snell's shoulder. Suddenly, halfway up, Jeanette halted.

'Where is Charlotte Penfield?' cried she.

'I saw her slip from the room,' declared Robert Mason.

'It's no matter,' grunted the Constable. 'She can do no harm.'

'Ah, but she is a wicked woman,' exclaimed Jeanette indignantly. 'She should be captured and hanged.'

'Yes, I agree,' smiled the Constable, 'but she is not worth looking for at the moment.'

'Do not fret yourself, Jeanette,' advised

Dick. 'She will be caught in due course.'

'Huh!' replied the girl and she continued up the stairs. They entered the hall and Hatchley went to look for Benjamin Tapner. Palmer was feeling stronger now and he left Will Snell and joined Jeanette, and they stood a little apart from the others, close together.

Hatchley soon returned with the ancient groomsman who by the smell of him, had been quaffing ale. 'Eh? What d'you want?' he cried.

'We want a stagecoach,' Pucky replied, 'to take three of us to the village.'

Benjamin Tapner eyed the Chief Constable speculatively. Then he exclaimed: 'Ay, I think that can be arranged. Stir not, it will be ready before you can blink an eye.' With that he trundled off across the hall and disappeared.

'What about the Squire's men in the cellar?' asked Palmer.

'We three will stay behind,' replied the Constable, nodding at Mason and Hatchley. 'We'll escort them to Loughton later.'

'Take care,' warned Palmer. 'They will

know what their punishment will be and, I fancy, try any trick to escape.'

'Don't worry,' grunted the Constable, 'we will take care.'

'What about our steeds?' asked Will Snell.

'Oh,' replied Pucky, 'let me see — we will bring them along later.'

There came the sound of creaking wheels and the clatter of horses' hooves and the Squire's coach rolled into view and halted at the front door. Jeanette, Will Snell and Dick Palmer walked out and clambered aboard.

'Farewell,' called the Constable.

Benjamin Tapner, in the driver's seat, raised the whip. But suddenly Timothy Pucky called out again. 'Hold!' he cried.

The old groomsman cursed, lowered his whip and turned round and glared at the Constable. Pucky ran down the steps of the manor and over to the side of the coach and leaned in through the window. He glanced at Dick Palmer and then at Will Snell with a grin on his red countenance.

'All is forgotten,' he whispered.

Dick's and Will's eyes lighted up. 'Ah, Constable,' Dick replied sincerely, 'that is indeed good of you — many thanks.'

Pucky stepped back and waved his hand and Benjamin Tapner gave a great crack to the whip and the sound echoed about the walls of Wake Manor as the coach lurched forward and trundled off down the drive on its way to the Black Horse Inn.

19

The coach creaked and groaned as it bumped along the old Epping Road and up on top Benjamin Tapner whistled to himself in a right merry manner. Inside, Jeanette, Dick and Will were silent, for they were very tired.

Will noticed that Dick sat in a somewhat stiff attitude and there was a pale, drawn look upon his face. The young highwayman's wound was painful and the rocking of the coach did not help matters. Will glanced across at Jeanette and realised that she, too, was in pain. She sat on the edge of the wooden seat her back well away from the back of the coach and her head bent forward so that her black tresses hung down over her bosom. Now and again the coach lurched wildly and the girl was thrown against the back of the seat, and every time this occurred an agonised expression passed over her features.

Palmer also noticed Jeanette's plight and he moved closer to her, placed his uninjured arm around her waist and steadied her. Thus she was able to relax and in a little while her head slipped sideways on to his shoulder, and for the time being they both forgot their discomfiture and were happy.

Will Snell stared out of the window into the night. Once through a gap in the trees he saw the moon bright and full low down in the sky and he realised that it was far past midnight. The storm was over and a clear, starlit world now replaced the heavy black clouds that had hung over the landscape earlier in the evening.

The only sign of life that greeted the coach as it swung into the village was a single yellow light that twinkled from the open doorway of the Black Horse Inn. As they drew nearer Will Snell observed two figures standing at the door silhouetted against the light from behind. The coach skidded to a halt to the accompaniment of lurid oaths from Benjamin Tapner.

Emily and Harry Murray, for it was

they, rushed forward anxiously. Will Snell
jumped out and Dick Palmer followed
more slowly. They turned and assisted
Jeanette to the ground. Emily, upon
seeing the girl, gave a shrill cry of delight
and flung her arms about her. With a gasp
of pain Jeanette shrank away.

'Her back is hurt,' Will Snell explained
quietly. He turned to Harry Murray. 'I
think you had better fetch Doctor Slater;
Dick is injured too.'

The landlord nodded and without
waiting to ask any questions hurried off
across the green to one of the cottages
upon the far side. Emily led the way into
the inn and Dick and Will followed,
supporting Jeanette. When they reached
the back Emily took the girl's arm herself
and helped her along the passage and up
the narrow staircase to her bedroom.

As they went up Jeanette whispered
something in Emily's ear and the woman
stopped and called back over her
shoulder:

'Dick — Will Snell — your bedroom is
at the end of the passage up here.'

'Oh, thank you, Madam, thank you,'

Wild Will called back. 'That is kind of you.' The two men settled down in the parlour and in a little while there came the sound of footsteps in the passage outside. Harry Murray entered the room accompanied by a short, plump man — Peter Slater, the village doctor.

'Well, let us have a look at it, me lad,' he cried, upon seeing Palmer. 'Let us have a look at it. I'll soon do you and then I can see Jeanette.'

Dick held out his arm and the doctor pulled up his sleeve and inspected the wound. Slater grunted and delved into his bag and produced a pot of cream, some lint and a bandage.

These he soon applied and a minute later Palmer's arm was bandaged up neatly and firmly.

'It's only a flesh wound, me lad,' Slater exclaimed. 'It'll be as right as rain in a day or two. Now then,' he added, 'where's the second patient?'

'If you will kindly follow me, doctor,' replied the landlord, 'I will show you. She's upstairs.'

Slater nodded and they left the room.

Dick Palmer collapsed in a chair and waited anxiously for the doctor's return. Nearly half an hour passed by and there was no sign of the man. Not a sound came from the room above and Dick grew more worried. He sat very still staring straight ahead, his fingers clutching the arms of the chair. Will Snell, meanwhile, walked restlessly up and down the room, for he, too, was a little anxious.

At last they heard the doctor's light footsteps on the stairs and then he appeared in the doorway of the parlour. Dick Palmer leapt from his chair. 'Well?' he cried.

Slater grinned. 'Ah, me lad, she'll be all right, don't worry. The wounds are nasty but they will heal and I doubt whether any sign will be left. She must stay in bed for a week or so, though.'

Palmer sighed with relief and Will Snell stopped pacing the room.

'Thank God for that,' Dick Palmer breathed.

'And talking of bed,' added the doctor, 'that is where I am off to now. Goodnight all.' He packed his little bag and was gone.

Harry Murray turned to the two men. 'Emily says she has told you where your bedroom is. It's late and you both look weary. Come! Let us get some sleep.'

The three left the room and made their way upstairs. As soon as they were shown their room Will and Dick collapsed upon their beds and were soon fast asleep. Quiet settled down on the Black Horse Inn and the son of Dick Turpin slept peacefully in the village of High Beach.

On the morrow Will Snell and Dick Palmer rose and descended to the parlour and there consumed a large breakfast. Jeanette still slept, Harry Murray informed Dick, but she already had a bit of colour in her cheeks and her breathing was steady and undisturbed. After the meal Dick and Will assisted the landlord with his many tasks about the inn.

The morning was well advanced when there came a loud knock upon the kitchen door. Emily Murray was upstairs at the time and so Dick answered the summons. Standing on the doorstep, a large grin upon his cherubic countenance, was the Chief Constable.

'Top 'o the mornin' to you, Dick,' cried he.

'Morning to you,' replied Dick with a smile. 'Step inside and tell us your news.'

The Constable, looking very smart in his black coat and waistcoat, strode through to the parlour and, on seeing Will Snell sprawled in the armchair, cried: 'Hello, Tiny, how are you?'

'Greetings, Constable,' replied Will. 'At the moment I am very weary; these barrels of ale are no light weight.'

'What!' cried Pucky. 'Why they should be easy for such as you.'

'Huh,' replied Will. He added: 'You seem mighty happy this bright morning.'

'That I am,' the Constable replied. 'I have those three villains under safe lock and key.'

'You are sure they are safe?' asked Palmer with a twinkle in his eye.

'Safe as if they were in Newgate jail itself,' exclaimed the Constable with a loud laugh. 'I have had two new sturdy bars put in that window.' He turned to

Will Snell. 'Not even you could break them.'

'Is that a challenge?' asked Will.

'Ah, no,' smiled the Constable.

'Doesn't matter,' grunted the giant. 'I have no wish to. They can rot in there for all I care.'

At that moment Emily Murray entered the parlour. 'Good morning, Constable,' she greeted.

'Good morning, my lady,' replied Pucky. 'How is the girl?'

'She is progressing rapidly,' Emily informed him. 'Doctor Slater says she must stay in bed for a week or two.'

'Of course — make certain of her complete recovery.'

'Please excuse me,' Emily added, 'but I have much work to do.' She disappeared into the kitchen.

Pucky turned to Dick Palmer. 'I see you are not troubled with your arm.'

'No, it was merely a flesh wound.'

'Good!' exclaimed the Constable. 'By the way,' he added in a more serious tone, 'one reason for my visit this morning was to repeat my words to you of last night:

you two gentlemen, as far as I am concerned, are as free as the air. I have no charge against you.'

Dick Palmer bowed. 'I thank you most sincerely, Constable Pucky,' he replied quietly.

Emily Murray appeared in the doorway again. This time she held a tray in her hands and upon the tray were three glasses of cordial. 'There you are,' she said, placing the tray on the table, and then she went out again.

'What a thoughtful woman,' said Pucky.

'This is an occasion,' cried Will Snell, jumping to his feet. 'A toast, Dick to our friend the Constable here. May he lead a contented and well-filled life.'

'Hear, hear,' said Palmer, and together they drank the health of Timothy Pucky.

The Constable bowed solemnly. 'Thank you my good friends,' he replied. 'That reminds me,' he added. 'The whole village, I see, already knows the story about the Squire. As I came into the inn there were many gossiping crowds standing about the green.'

'Quite believe it,' Palmer commented.

'Mark my words,' the Constable declared with raised finger, 'all London will have heard tell of the Squire of Wake Manor before many a day is past.'

A few days later the two highwaymen had reason to remember the Constable's forecast. The story of Adam Penfield's wild scheme and the resultant discovery that Jeanette Murray was in reality his daughter became the talk of the countryside, and many were the strangers that appeared in the village, wandered curiously about and stared inquisitively at everybody and everything. Many also were the eyewitness accounts that suddenly became available from the villagers for the gratification of these intruders. The Black Horse Inn did a roaring trade.

Jeanette in two weeks' time was out and about as fresh and as lovely as ever. She and Dick kept well out of the way of the many 'seekers of knowledge' and they often wandered into the forest to the little glade during the warm summer days and no one could find them.

Will Snell in the meantime helped the landlord in the inn and in the evenings kept order in the bar, for with the growing trade it became full of strange faces and there was much noise and ribald merriment. Directly Will's great figure appeared on the scene, however, the shouting and the singing died away and was replaced by a respectful hum.

'Nay, Will,' Harry Murray exclaimed thankfully one evening, 'as things are now I don't know what I should do without you.'

'It's a pleasure,' boomed Will. 'I am taking a liking for the job.'

Such was the state of things in the village when, one day in the late afternoon some weeks after the night of the fight at Wake Manor, there rode into High Beach on a fine white courser a dusty traveller. But he was not one of the usual curious visitors; that the villagers knew immediately.

The dust could not conceal the fineness of the traveller's clothes and his tired appearance did not detract from his important bearing, and excited whispers fluttered around High Beach. The new-comer trotted up to the Black Horse Inn and a small, wide-eyed crowd appeared as if from nowhere and followed him at a distance. He dismounted wearily and walked up to the door of the inn and knocked loudly.

Both Emily and Harry had observed the commotion from the bar window the traveller's arrival had caused, and it was with some trepidation and wonder that they answered the summons together.

'Yes, sir?' asked the landlord, a little hesitantly.

'Are you,' asked the traveller in a pompous manner, 'Mr. Harry Murray, landlord of the Black Horse Inn?'

'I am,' replied Harry, with some anxiety in his voice.

'Then,' declared the traveller, 'I wish to speak to your protégé, Miss Jeanette Martilliére Penfield.'

20

A hushed silence followed the stranger's words and for a moment Harry Murray could only stare at him blankly. Emily's mouth dropped open in a rather vacant manner. An excited murmur rose from the little crowd of villagers.

Emily at last turned away from the newcomer and looked up at her husband, who was trying to think of something to say. 'They are out at the back,' she whispered to him.

The landlord nodded, but he was not going to be hurried. 'What is it you wish to see her about?' he asked stoutly squaring his shoulders.

'I have an important personal message for her,' replied the man haughtily.

The landlord gave a heavy grunt but still, to show that he was not afraid or the slightest bit impressed by the well-dressed visitor, he turned about in a leisurely manner and sauntered off down the passage. When he reached the yard at the back, however, Harry quickened his pace and rushed across to the gap between the stables at the edge of the forest. He peered about the trees and bushes but could see nothing. It would be futile to enter and look for Jeanette and Dick, so he stood still and listened. But it was of no use — the twitter of the birds, an odd animal cry and the faint rustle of the trees were all the sounds that he could hear.

At last he cried out in a loud voice: 'Jeanette, Dick, where are you?'

There was a short silence, then the landlord heard Dick Palmer's voice reply from deep in the forest: 'Yes, Harry, what is it?'

'Come here,' shouted the landlord. 'It's important.'

In a few moments Jeanette and Dick appeared from out of the forest, their hands clasped, their faces radiant. They halted before the landlord and stared at him questioningly. 'Well Harry, what's all the fuss?' asked Dick cheerfully.

'There's a visitor just arrived in the

village,' said the landlord in an excited tone. 'He's asking for you, Jeanette — he spoke your new name, Jeanette Martilliére Penfield!'

The girl's hand flew to her lips and she gave a startled gasp. She turned and gazed up at Dick Palmer. He smiled reassuringly at her and then looked at Harry Murray. 'Where is this fellow?'

'At the front of the inn,' replied the landlord.

'Come, then, let us see what he has to say.'

Together the three of them hurried across the yard and entered the house. There was an excited gleam in Jeanette's eyes and she almost ran down the passage, pulling Palmer along behind her. They arrived at the door and there found Will Snell and Emily Murray standing facing the messenger in awkward silence. The latter was now completely surrounded by the inquisitive villagers. He had struck an elegant, rather lofty pose and was tapping one foot impatiently upon the cobbled stones.

At sight of Jeanette, however, he was

somewhat taken aback — he had not expected such a lovely young woman.

Jeanette came to a breathless halt before him. 'Yes?' she cried, gazing at him with shining, dark eyes.

The messenger coughed and glanced down quickly at the ground to regain his composure. When he looked up again his manner had changed and he now spoke in a respectful, almost gallant, tone.

'Mademoiselle,' cried he, 'forgive me for disturbing you this pleasant afternoon, but I have just arrived from London and carry with me an important letter addressed to you from the trustees of the Martilliére estate.'

At this a gasp went up from the villagers and Jeanette's heart beat a little quicker. Dick Palmer remained stern, however, and waited for the messenger to continue. The man was quite pleased with the commotion he had caused and he turned round and frowned down upon the villagers. He faced Jeanette again and opened a small pouch attached to his belt, and withdrew a sheet of paper. This he handed to the girl and then stood back respectfully. A thrilled twitter ran through the villagers,

Jeanette opened the note and read it in silence, all eyes upon her. A hush settled on the throng. When she had finished she handed the paper to Dick without a word. The highwayman read it through carefully.

The letter was from a firm of London solicitors, Messrs Hargin and Hargincourt, of Chancery Lane, Agents for Messrs Jean Raviare and Pierre Joblet, of Paris. It was rather a lengthy composition and not worth detailing here. In effect it said that the Martilliére fortune was now in their, the solicitors' hands, and if she, 'the absolute heir to the jewels heirlooms and a 'certain sum of money',' would deign to call upon them at their offices at some future date, following the signing and the completion of certain necessary documents, the said fortune would be transferred into her possession.

'Thank you kindly,' Jeanette said to the messenger. 'Tell Mr. Hargin we will visit him at his offices within a few weeks.' She turned then and clutched Dick's arm.

The messenger glanced quickly from one to the other then bowed suddenly, stepped back and walked slowly away to his horse. The villagers opened up to let him pass through and, when he was clear, surged forward again around Jeanette and Dick. The messenger mounted his horse, dug in his spurs and cantered off down the road.

Dick Palmer handed the letter to Harry Murray and he and Emily read it together, their eyes widening with wonder as the full meaning of the message was brought home to them. For a second Emily looked a little sad but she soon changed when she saw how happy and excited were Jeanette and Dick.

Will Snell read the letter out loud to himself with ponderous pauses and heavy gasps, so that the villagers found him hard to follow.

'Let's go inside,' suggested Jeanette, and she led the way into the inn. The villagers were left standing outside gaping after them with frustrated annoyance, for they were still not sure of what exactly was going on.

Jeanette, Dick, Will and Harry entered the parlour and Emily went into the kitchen and made some tea. Then they all sat in a circle in the parlour and discussed the great news. They talked of the future and of what they would do with the money, depending on how much it was. After a while, however, the conversation waned and suddenly Emily jumped up and, pulling Harry and Will after her, left the room.

Jeanette and Dick sat in silence for several moments after they had gone. At last Jeanette rose. 'Let us go to the glade,' she suggested.

Dick Palmer nodded and he put his arm around her waist and they crossed the yard and entered the forest. They reached the glade and sat down on the bank where they had often sat before. They moved close to one another, and the birds in the trees above them sang merrily.

All of a sudden memories of the past came flooding back to Palmer. He remembered his first visit to this glade and of the surprise attack by Timothy

Pucky and his men; and he remembered that it was here, too, that Jeanette and he had discovered the hollow mounting in her ring. All his adventures since he first arrived in High Beach flashed through his mind. All the amazing and apparently disconnected events of the past had now fallen into place and everything seemed quite straightforward.

Dick Palmer turned to the girl at his side and they smiled happily at one another, and he took her gently in his arms.

THE END

*Books by John Russell Fearn
in the Linford Mystery Library:*

THE TATTOO MURDERS
VISION SINISTER
THE SILVERED CAGE
WITHIN THAT ROOM!
REFLECTED GLORY
THE CRIMSON RAMBLER
SHATTERING GLASS
THE MAN WHO WAS NOT
ROBBERY WITHOUT VIOLENCE
DEADLINE
ACCOUNT SETTLED
STRANGER IN OUR MIDST
WHAT HAPENED TO HAMMOND?
THE GLOWING MAN
FRAMED IN GUILT
FLASHPOINT
THE MASTER MUST DIE
DEATH IN SILHOUETTE
THE LONELY ASTRONOMER
THY ARM ALONE
MAN IN DUPLICATE
THE RATTENBURY MYSTERY

CLIMATE INCORPORATED
THE FIVE MATCHBOXES
EXCEPT FOR ONE THING
BLACK MARIA, M.A.
ONE STEP TOO FAR
THE THIRTY-FIRST OF JUNE
THE FROZEN LIMIT
ONE REMAINED SEATED
THE MURDERED SCHOOLGIRL